D1509979

Jodie's Journey

COLIN THIELE

Jodie's Journey

HARPER & ROW, PUBLISHERS, NEW YORK
Grand Rapids, Philadelphia, St. Louis, San Francisco
London, Singapore, Sydney, Tokyo, Toronto

Jodie's Journey
Copyright © 1988 by Colin Thiele
First published by Walter McVitty Books,
27 Hereford Street, Glebe, NSW 2037, Australia
1   2   3   4   5   6   7   8   9   10
First American Edition, 1990

Library of Congress Cataloging-in-Publication Data
Thiele, Colin.
     Jodie's journey/Colin Thiele.
        p.   cm.
     Summary: Twelve-year-old Jodie, disabled by juvenile rheumatoid
arthritis and no longer able to ride her beloved horse Monarch, faces a
crisis when the two of them are alone at her remote Australian home
and a devastating fire approaches.
     ISBN 0-06-026132-3—ISBN 0-06-026133-1 (lib. bdg.)
     [1. Rheumatoid arthritis—Fiction.   2. Physically handicapped—
Fiction.   3. Horses—Fiction.   4. Fires—Fiction.   5. Australia—
Fiction.]   I. Title.
PZ7.T354Jo   1990   90-4072
[Fic]—dc20   CIP
                                                                    AC

For
Sharyn Stevens

Jodie's Journey

1

JODIE CARPENTER was in the middle of her final round in the Greenvale Junior Show Jumping Championship. She was riding Monarch against the clock. He had cleared the first four jumps easily but at the fifth he veered slightly and clipped the top rail. For a terrible moment she held her breath, expecting to hear the rail rattle and thump as it fell to the ground behind her. But there was nothing more. She couldn't resist a lightning glance over her left shoulder to make sure that it was still in place, even though the constantly repeated words of Oscar Hoffmann, her riding instructor, were ringing in her ears: "Never look back. It interferes with the balance of the horse and upsets

3

your line of ride. Whether the rail is up or down, there's nothing you can do about it anymore. Concentrate on the next jump."

Jodie concentrated. Number Six was a nasty double—two jumps arranged within a few yards of each other and counting as one. It was set at an angle to Number Five. It was meant to test the riders by forcing them into a hard decision: whether to play safe by going around wide and giving the horse time to straighten up, or to take a big risk by turning short and coming in at an angle, trying to save five or six seconds.

Jodie decided to go wide. There was no point in saving time if you lost a rail in the process. She was the last rider in the competition. There were already two others with clear rounds ahead of her, so she had to go clear at all costs to gain a place. She would have to depend on Monarch's speed later in the round to have any hope of finishing in the fastest time.

As they came up to the double, Monarch lost his stride slightly, and for a heart-stopping second, Jodie thought he was going to blunder straight into the first of the jumps. But he corrected himself beautifully, just cleared the top rail, regained his rhythm, and sailed over the second without mishap. Jodie breathed more easily.

Number Seven was an imitation brick wall with a high rounded top. It was a demanding jump—the sort of solid-looking barrier that Monarch always hated. She had to ride him hard to prevent him from balking, but her urging seemed to get his dander up and he thundered forward like a maniac, jumped too soon, rose high into the air, and just grazed the top of the wall as he came down. Two sections were jolted out of position slightly but neither of them fell.

"Lucky twit," said Amanda Ritchie to her friend Jessica Hollis at the side of the arena. Amanda disliked Jodie because she was her main rival at most of the shows. Amanda's horse, Superior, had gone clear earlier in the afternoon and was leading the competition. She didn't want Jodie Carpenter beating her at the last minute, as she often did.

Jodie was not even aware of Amanda or any of the other people who were watching. She was looking too intently at Number Eight, now looming up ahead—a wide brush fence with crossbars. But all went well. Monarch sailed over it like Pegasus. It should have boosted her confidence, but her stomach was still tied up in knots and her heartbeat was thumping in her ears. She sensed that Monarch was beginning to enjoy himself. He was a lovely little thoroughbred, a bay gelding with a narrow white blaze on his nose. He was only just fifteen hands, but on a good day he seemed to have springs in his legs and rockets in his hoofs.

Number Nine was on the far side of the course, fifty or sixty yards away. Jodie let him have his head, and they flew across the oval to make up time.

"He's a fast little horse," said old Bert Martin, taking the cigarette out of his mouth with yellow nicotine-stained fingers.

His neighbor, Fred Lang, agreed. "Darts about like a ferret."

"Can jump too."

"When he's in the mood."

Jodie reined Monarch back as they approached Number Nine, in case he tried to do too much. She need not have worried. He cleared the jump in his stride and galloped on beautifully. But the round was still far from over, and a few seconds later they faced the biggest test of all. Number Ten was a triple, set fairly close in, so there wasn't much time to prepare for it. Monarch was all for charging forward regardless. Jodie tried desperately to settle him down, straining on the reins. Her arms ached and there was a biting pain in her hands where the skin over her knuckles was stretched taut. The horse seemed to understand, and steadied at the last second without losing his impetus. In the grandstand her father and mother held their breath.

"This is it," her father said, watching intently through his binoculars.

Her mother was biting her lip without being aware of it. "I can't bear to watch," she said.

"One," he called under his breath as Jodie and Monarch cleared the first jump.

"Two," he added even more breathlessly an instant later. "Go, go, go; don't lose your rhythm!"

Monarch had faltered fractionally between the second and third elements but Jodie had ridden him well. His nostrils were wide and his eyes bulged as if he knew that he faced the most critical jump of his life.

"Three!" Mr. Carpenter yelled the word. "She's made it!"

There were cheers, shouts, and a spatter of applause all around the grounds.

Now only two jumps remained, both fairly straightforward, designed to give the competitors a good run down to the finishing line. Jodie dug in her heels and clapped on speed. Monarch fairly raced around the arena.

Andy Schulz, the timekeeper, was watching the stopwatch in his hand. "She's got twelve seconds," he said to Tony Chapple, the chief judge. "She just might do it."

Monarch bore down on Number Eleven, arched up and over, and was galloping on again in the blink of an eye.

"She *will* do it," Andy said. "I reckon she'll win."

"If she doesn't pull a rail at the last jump," Tony answered. "They often do, you know. Get carried away and jump too soon."

"I can't bear to watch," Mrs. Carpenter said for the fifth time that day. "Tell me when it's over."

Mr. Carpenter seemed to be talking into his binoculars. "Here she comes."

Monarch was streaking toward Number Twelve. Jodie was riding well forward in the saddle, her mind in such a turmoil of anxiety and excitement that she scarcely knew whether she was still in control or whether Monarch had taken over and was finishing the course on his own.

"Steady, steady," Mr. Carpenter murmured. His breath was fogging up the lenses on the binoculars. "Hold him. Hold him."

Jodie admitted afterward that it was luck rather than good riding that brought Monarch up to the last jump with a perfectly judged stride. In spite of his speed he took off at exactly the right point, just cleared the top rail in a low flat arc, and landed smoothly like a champion hurdler.

"She's clear. She's clear," Mr. Carpenter yelled.

A moment later Monarch hurtled across the finish line amid a bedlam of shouts, cheers, and honking car horns.

"She's done it!" Andy Schulz cried excitedly. "She's two seconds clear of the field."

Jodie pulled up fifty yards farther on and leaned forward, patting Monarch ecstatically on the neck. "Good boy," was all she could gasp out over and over again. "Good boy. Good boy."

Monarch, with his flanks heaving and his nostrils spuming, seemed to agree. He opened his mouth on the bit with what looked almost like a grin.

Jodie's father and mother and her friend Tanya Thompson came rushing over. "Congratulations," they called. "Well done. Marvelous."

Tanya was overjoyed for Jodie's sake. She didn't have a horse of her own, and so she idolized Monarch and acted as Jodie's groom. In return Jodie often let her have a ride. "You were wonderful, Jode," she cried. "Magic. You deserved to win."

Shortly afterward the winners were called to receive their ribbons and trophies, and Jodie had to lead the little cavalcade across the oval. Horses and

9

riders stood in a line in front of the grandstand full of clapping people while the details of their times and placings were announced over the loud-speakers. Then Tony Chapple stepped forward and pinned the shining blue ribbon around Monarch's neck, shook hands with Jodie, and handed her the winner's prize—a silver-plated model horse mounted on a stand, and a check for a hundred dollars.

It was the most wonderful moment in Jodie's life. For her, the whole world seemed to sing with joy. The sky seemed brighter and the sunshine more golden than it had ever been. As she trotted out of the arena, she had to let Monarch follow his head, because tears blurred her eyes.

Even Amanda Ritchie's jealousy couldn't dim her joy. "Bit clumsy; clipped three rails but none of them fell."

Jodie smiled and said nothing. She looked at the blue ribbon around Monarch's neck and hugged her happiness to herself. It was a moment that nothing could ever take away from her.

2

WHEN JODIE woke up next morning, her wrists were stiff and her knuckles hurt terribly. It was a pain that she had suffered on and off for more than a year, although nobody had taken much notice of it. They put it down to "growing pains" or a sprain. Once her mother had taken down an old tin of camphorated ointment and rubbed it on Jodie's wrists. It had made her smell like an ancient wardrobe strewn with moth-balls, but it hadn't done her any good. She complained about it again at breakfast, but her mother just smiled at her kindly and said, "I'm not surprised, the way you were hanging on to Monarch in the arena yesterday."

11

"But I had to."

"I thought he was going to tear your arms out."

Jodie's father looked up from the piece of toast he was trying to spread with apple jelly. The jelly tended to wobble all over the place and drop off the spoon before he could get it out of the jar. "You rode with a very tight rein, you know."

"But there's no other way. Not with Monarch."

"Ossie Hoffmann is forever telling you to relax."

"That's all very well for him to say."

At that moment Jodie's big brother, Alan, walked in. He was almost seven years older than she was. During the week he stayed down in Adelaide with friends while he went to the university, so they rarely saw him except on weekends. He called Jodie his kid sister and still regarded her as a little girl. "The trouble with you is that you're just a pimple," he said, "and Monarch's a fair-sized pumpkin."

In a way he was right. Her twelfth birthday was still a week or two off, and she was small for her age. But she pouted at Alan's comment all the same. "I can ride him better than anyone. Ossie Hoffmann says so."

Alan poured himself a cup of coffee. "Maybe you can, but he's still a handful."

"We understand each other, Monarch and me. We're soul mates."

12

Her father rolled his eyes. Girls and horses! It was a form of addiction. Once a girl started riding, she became hopelessly hooked on it. That was really why they had left the city and moved out to a little twenty-five–acre farm near Greenvale, in the Adelaide Hills. It was a lovely spot, although they seldom seemed to have time to appreciate it.

He wondered whether Jodie overdid things. She had to get up early every morning, feed Monarch, gulp down her breakfast, catch the school bus at eight, spend all day at school, come home at four thirty, lunge Monarch and work him in the menage — the makeshift practice arena they had cleared in the scrub near the house — wash him down and brush him afterward, muck out his stable, give him his feed and water, clean herself up and have tea, do her homework, and finally tumble into bed. It was a long hard day. And it went on like that week after week and month after month.

"My fingers are so sore I can hardly bend them," Jodie was saying, "and my knuckles hurt like mad. They're all swollen."

Her mother didn't seem greatly concerned. "You probably wrenched them at one of the jumps."

"My knees hurt too."

Her father was munching the toast he'd finally

managed to spread with jelly. "From digging them in, I guess."

"You'd better have an easy day," her mother said. "Just relax. You'll soon feel better."

Her father stretched and yawned. "That's exactly what I'm going to do. I've declared it a do-nothing day."

Alan was frying himself four eggs and three slices of bacon. "No rest for me," he grumbled. "I've got to finish an essay for old Baldy Straitjacket."

Jodie looked up in astonishment. "Who?"

Her father glanced at his son in distaste. "Professor Ironsides to you."

Alan put two big slabs of toast on his plate and piled the eggs and bacon on top of them. His mother looked at the mess in disgust. "Don't they feed you down there during the week?"

"Haven't got time to eat. Life's too hectic."

His father grunted. "You can say that again." He worked for a big city firm and was forever traveling in one part of the state or another — the South East, the Riverland, the West Coast, even as far away as Broken Hill. He was away more often than he was home.

Jodie's mother was always busy too. She worked part-time in the Burnside Library, which meant driving down to town on most days. In addition, she was secretary or president of half a dozen clubs and committees that kept on having endless meetings.

"Thank heaven for Sundays," Jodie's father said, stretching hugely again. "And Saturdays too, for that matter."

"Oh yes, Saturdays are very restful," her mother answered tartly. "Watching people risk their necks on wild horses."

"Ahhh, Mum." Jodie was going to protest hotly but she could see that her mother had half a smile on her face.

It was true, of course. Saturdays were hectic too. Usually they were out at dawn working in a frenzy — loading the car, hitching on the horse trailer, coaxing Monarch aboard, grabbing saddles and bridles, and packing a hundred things ranging from riding jodhpurs to biscuits, hay to hoof oil. Then there was the urgent drive to the show of the day or the Pony Club meet — at Murray Bridge or Mount Pleasant, Gawler or Strathalbyn, Angaston in the Barossa Valley or even at Greenvale itself. They had to make sure they arrived in time for Monarch to be given a good workout before the first event.

And in the evening it all had to be done in reverse. Often it was dark by the time they got back home. Then they had to blunder about in the yard, unloading and stabling Monarch, unhitching the trailer, and carrying mountains of gear inside. They were usually dead tired, and sometimes cold and wet as well. But Jodie knew that she could never give up riding. Such an idea was impossible for her to contemplate.

In spite of her mother's hope for a restful day, things didn't work out that way. After lunch there was a phone call to say that their neighbor, Mrs. Lang, had had a bad fall. Her husband was in a tizzy. Could Jodie's mother come over quickly to look after the baby while they rushed off to the hospital? She had barely left when Alan announced that he had to go back to town because he needed some books from the university library to finish his essay. And Jodie's father found that he had some important paperwork to do. He had to set out for Port Augusta at six o'clock the next morning.

Jodie went down to the stables. She had to clean up properly after yesterday's outing and get things ready for the coming week. She didn't feel well. When she used the big wheelbarrow, the pain in her knuckles was so bad that the handles almost slipped from her grip. She had to grit her teeth and clench her hands to manage it.

Her knees hurt too, and so did her hips. She tried to remember whether she had jarred her body sharply a week or two back when Monarch had reared suddenly and thrown her in the menage, but surely that couldn't have caused the pain she was feeling now.

She struggled on, mucking out the stall, cleaning the feed bin, emptying and refilling the water trough, tidying the gear, and sorting and hanging up bridles, halters, and ropes.

Finally she gave Monarch twenty minutes on the lunging rein to work off any stiffness from the hard competition he'd been through. She wanted to give him a light workout in the menage too, but by now her hands and her right knee were hurting so much that she couldn't bear the thought.

She was glad that the show jumping season was almost at an end. She would soon be spelling Monarch for a month or two during the summer recess, which really meant that she would be giving herself a spell too. If the pain in her joints was being caused by the strain and pressure of her riding, then perhaps the damage would have time to heal while she was out of the saddle.

That night she took some aspirin and went to bed early.

3

A T SCHOOL the next day Jodie was a star. Mr.
Gladstone, the principal, congratulated her
in front of the whole assembly, and Mr.
Harrison, her teacher, asked her to talk to the class
about grooming and caring for horses.

In the yard at recess time, as she and Tanya sat
sharing an apple, dozens of their schoolmates came
up to talk about Jodie's win. They did it in all kinds
of ways.

"It was a magic ride, Jodie. . . ."

"Can I borrow your horse, Carpo?"

"What about a loan, moneybags?"

Jodie beamed. Because she was so small—"like

a dark-haired little gypsy girl," old Bert Martin used to say — she had never stood out in sports or leadership at school. It was nice to be top dog for a change, to be seen as a winner. She basked in the glow of it.

Only Amanda Ritchie and a few members of her clique failed to congratulate her. "I don't know how she does it," Amanda said loudly, talking with her head in the air. There was a brief pause. Everyone was silent, wondering what she meant, which was exactly what Amanda wanted so that she could attract attention. "I reckon she puts glue on the rails to stop them from falling."

Although Amanda was a big girl, it seemed for a moment that Jodie was going to fly at her. Her dark eyes shone angrily. "Some riders are just plain clumsy," she answered sarcastically. It was a barbed reference to one of Amanda's recent rides when she had spread-eagled most of the jumps on the course.

Amanda's lip curled. "And like I said, some people are just plain clumsy."

Tanya stood up at that. She was tall and blond, with blue eyes and fair skin, like a girl from Sweden or Norway. "Look, Amanda," she said, "why don't you just shove it. If you're jealous of Jodie, then go and cry in a bucket." It was a comment that was too honest and too forthright for Amanda. She huffed in disdain and walked away.

For the rest of the week Jodie was still on top of the world. On Saturday she had a lovely party for her twelfth birthday. Tanya, Lynn Abbott, and two or three other close friends stayed on and slept overnight, talking in bed until two o'clock in the morning and then sleeping in luxuriously. But the soreness in Jodie's hands and the pain in her knees and hips didn't improve. She felt achy and out of sorts.

Early the next week, when things still hadn't improved, her mother decided to take her to the doctor. "It's about time you had a really good check-up," she said. Dr. Manners, their local G.P., was a kindly old man with gray hair and gold-rimmed glasses. He shared the clinic in Greenvale with Dr. Simpson. Between them they knew every man, woman, child, and baby in the Hills for a dozen miles around, because they had been in the district for so long.

Dr. Manners greeted them warmly. "Hullo, Helen. Hullo, Jodie, I hear you're a champion rider these days." People said he had such perfect bed-side manners that long ago he had been nicknamed

"Dr. Bedside" and the name had stuck — so much so that several newcomers to Greenvale thought it was his real name and used it when they called at the clinic. He thought this was so hilariously funny that he kept telling the story to everyone he met.

Jodie's mother chatted with him for a minute or two, and then he folded his hands on the desk in front of him and smiled at Jodie. "Well now," he said, "what seems to be the problem?"

And so it began. It was all rather frightening — having to lie on a couch like someone in an operating room, having a stethoscope probing about on her chest and back, having her throat and ears explored, having her body kneaded here, there, and everywhere, having her joints manipulated, having to answer a stream of questions about the things she had been doing. Had she fallen from Monarch lately, or tumbled off her bike, or tripped at school? Had she accidentally knocked her knuckles against the edge of the desk, or bruised her knee against a post while riding? Had she had any spider bites or insect stings?

Jodie had the impression that Dr. Manners was being unnecessarily long-winded, but at last it was over and she was able to get dressed again and

21

join her mother in the outer office. Dr. Manners sat at his desk and told them he didn't think it was anything serious. He thought she had probably strained her wrists while riding, and bruised her knee in some way. She was burning up a lot of energy and perhaps overdoing it. If she rested for a while, things would settle down. The warm summer weather should help too.

Jodie's mother agreed. "That's what I thought." She turned toward Jodie. "There's only one more show, isn't there — before the end of the season?"

"Yes," Jodie answered, "at Emu Valley on Saturday. The Pony Club Cup."

Her mother nodded and looked at Dr. Manners. "Then Monarch can go out to grass and she can have a really good rest."

Dr. Manners finished writing some notes on a card and stood up. "Fine." He saw them politely to the door and smiled at Jodie. "Good luck for Saturday."

As they drove back home, Jodie's mother seemed greatly relieved. She chattered on and on as if the whole problem had been solved. Jodie didn't have the heart to tell her that Dr. Manners only seemed to have made things worse with the bending and twisting he had given her joints. They were hurting more than ever.

22

A few days later something happened at school that made Jodie unhappier still. In place of the normal physical education lessons, the teachers had arranged an afternoon of sport and class games on the oval. Everyone took part, and some of the parents and local people came along to watch. Toward the end of the day every class was divided into relay teams, with four runners in each group, to race around the oval. Luckily Jodie was allotted to Tanya Thompson's team, together with two boys, Sam Snell and Peter Hutchins. Peter was built like an athlete, but Sam was tiny — even smaller than Jodie. One of their rival teams consisted of Amanda Ritchie and Jessica Hollis, with two of their cronies.

As each group of teams raced off, there was a great deal of excited cheering. Spectators craned forward, friends on the sidelines jumped up and down on the spot, parents clapped and applauded. Teams that were still awaiting their turn went into secret huddles to decide the order in which their members would run. After a minute of confusion and debate Tanya's team chose Peter to run first, Sam second, and Jodie third, with Tanya herself covering the last lap to the finish line — she had a long loping stride and was certain to make up lost ground if necessary.

Amanda swaggered past just as they were preparing to take their places. "We'll be waiting for you at the finish line," she taunted.

Tanya was fed up with her. "Look, shove off, will you."

Amanda laughed. "What a team!" she scoffed. "We'll give you ten seconds' start. You'll need a handicap."

Shortly afterward Mr. Harrison lined up the starters, banged the gong he was using in place of a starting pistol, and sent them on their way.

Peter Hutchins did well. By the time he was ready to hand over the baton to Sam Snell, he was three yards clear of the other runners. They changed smoothly and Sam set off as fast as a startled rabbit. With his short legs racing and his small head bobbing, he looked like a rocketing clothespin.

"Come on, Sam! Come on, Sam!" people yelled enthusiastically.

Although he lost some ground, Sam was still a yard ahead of his nearest rivals when he reached Jodie for the next baton change. She had her hand ready as he approached, and he was holding up the baton to give her a clear grab at it. He was tiring badly, but he was still running fit to burst. The crowd yelled and cheered and Jodie's nerves were as taut as tension wire. She knew that if she could hold her own during the third stage, her team would win for certain. Nobody could beat Tanya over the last lap.

And then it happened. As little Sam came panting forward at the end of his run, his hand, clutching the baton, wavered about uncertainly. Jodie, who had already started moving forward, had to lunge at it, throwing all her weight on her right knee and twisting her wrist sharply. Sudden shafts of pain shot through her leg and arm. They were so intense that she gasped and checked herself momentarily. It caused her to fumble the baton for an agonizing second, and then it fell to the ground.

There was a groan of dismay from the spectators lined up at the side of the running track. ''Oh no, she's dropped the baton!''

Years afterward, when she was sometimes lying awake in bed, Jodie could still hear that accusing cry ringing in her head, over and over again. ''She's dropped the baton! She's dropped the baton!''

Although she stooped and picked it up in a flash, her team no longer had any hope of winning. She did her best, running with a limp because of the pain in her knee, and Tanya stormed home like an Olympian. But even Tanya couldn't make up the lost ground, and so they finished third. Jodie was so ashamed that she kept on apologizing to the others, but they just laughed and said it didn't really matter. It didn't make Jodie feel any better. She knew that it did matter.

To make things worse, Amanda's team had won. "What did I tell you?" she crowed.

Tanya glared at her. "Drop dead. We would have beaten you hands down if—" She stopped suddenly and bit her tongue.

"Well, if your team *will* drop the baton . . ." Amanda gave Jodie a superior look and walked away. "Some people are just frauds," she said to Jess Hollis, speaking loudly so that everyone could overhear her. "Limping around with long faces, pretending to have a sore leg. It's just a cover-up."

That was too much for Jodie. She hobbled over to the changing rooms by herself and burst into tears.

4

THE PAIN didn't go away. Instead, it grew worse. When Jodie went to board the school bus in the mornings, she had to clench her teeth as she tried to get up on the first high step in the doorway. Whether she pulled herself forward on the handrail or heaved herself up, one leg at a time, didn't really matter — either way the pain was excruciating.

At school it was clear that Mr. Harrison, her class teacher, had no idea of her problems. "Hurry up, Hopalong," he called impatiently when she came limping across the yard after recess, and then laughed at his own joke. "You're slower than winter treacle." It was a complete put-down, spoken without concern or understanding.

Later in the day he called her out to his table and pointed to a new piece of work she had written. "Look at this, Jodie." he said heavily. "The handwriting and setting out are dreadful. Your work has been getting worse and worse lately. How do you explain that?"

"It's my hands, Mr. Harrison. They hurt."

"Nonsense, Jodie, I'm sure they don't hurt *every* day."

She defended herself earnestly. "They do. They really do."

"Are you sure you're not exaggerating?"

She was appalled by the accusation. "No, Mr. Harrison. No. I'm not making it up."

He put the sheets down on the table with a sigh. "All right then." He looked at her skeptically. "But I'll be watching you, Jodie. I want a big effort between now and the end of the year."

She was flushed and angry as she limped back to her seat. His suspicion rankled. To be told that her written work was poor was bad enough, but to be accused of lying — for that's what it amounted to — was more than she could bear. At the back of the room Jess Hollis whispered and smirked. Jodie

28

gave her a withering glance and sat down. The sooner the year ended, the happier she would be. After Christmas she would be saying good-bye to Mr. Harrison forever and starting at Hillbank High School.

The last equestrian event of the year—the Pony Club Cup—was now only a few days away. Jodie tried to prepare for it as best she could. She lunged Monarch after school and gave him a workout in the menage, but the effort was exhausting. Just putting the saddle on his back was painful enough, and the effort of tightening the girth straps was unbearable—as if someone had poured gasoline over her wrists and then set fire to them. Even mixing the bran, oats, chaff, and molasses in his feed bin with her bare hands was agony.

Several times she stopped in her work, flicked the hair back from her face with a toss of her head, and looked at her hands. The knuckles were red and swollen. "It must be more than a sprain," she said to herself. "There has to be something wrong with them." Yet she was afraid to complain to her mother again for fear that she would forbid her to ride in the Pony Club Cup. It was an event she wanted to win. Coupled with the Greenvale

Championship, it would prove that she was the best junior rider of the year.

When they arrived at the Emu Valley showground on the following Saturday morning, she tried to hide her pain. She couldn't disguise her limp, but limps were common enough among riders because of falls, kicks, tight boots, sideswipes against posts, and even heavy horses accidentally stamping on toes. People tended not to take much notice.

Luckily Alan had come along for a change. He had almost finished his year at the university and had decided to take the weekend off. "I'll help Tanya and be your second groom, kiddo," he said breezily. "With me in the pits you can't lose."

She laughed. "It's not a motor race, you boof-head."

It was good to let him do most of the hard work — unloading, saddling, even giving her a hoist up. And so, as she prepared to give Monarch a brisk workout in the practice arena, nobody had any idea of the pain she was in. It was not until the bell had rung and she had actually started the course that people realized something was wrong.

After the first two jumps it was obvious. The thudding shock as Monarch took off and landed seemed to send barbs of pain into her arms and legs. Her fingers and wrists couldn't bear the pressure of the reins. It seemed to be pulling her hands apart. And so, as Monarch cleared the third jump, she released her grip on the left rein to try to get a moment's relief, although the right rein remained firm. She didn't do it consciously. It was almost as if her hand did it of its own accord. The effect was disastrous. Monarch misunderstood and veered to the right as he neared the next jump. Before Jodie could check him, he had swung away past the offside wing in a tight half circle. To the onlookers it seemed exactly like a refusal. A murmur of pity and dismay went up from the crowd. Jodie's father was surprised and disappointed. "What's got into him?" he said to Alan. "He rarely refuses, even when he doesn't like the look of the jump."

Out in the arena Jodie brought Monarch around as fast as she could, but the pain in her wrists was so intense that she simply couldn't control him. And he was clearly bewildered by the way she was handling the reins. He careered about uncertainly, charged at the jump, and then suddenly veered again. She wasn't prepared for it, and, because of the pain, she didn't have the power to hang on. As he darted aside, she went sailing over his near-side shoulder and landed on the ground in a heap.

"Ohhh." There was a cry around the oval, a kind of general indrawn breath.

"Is she all right?" Jodie's mother asked in a whisper. "I can't bear to look."

Tanya sprinted off to intercept Monarch as he galloped riderless across the arena. Alan and his father ran to help Jodie, who was getting up slowly, not because she had been hurt in the fall but because of the piercing pain in her knees and wrists. They reached her just as the commentator on the microphone decided that all was well. "She's okay," he announced, and there was a sigh of relief all around. "A bruise or two, maybe, but it looks as though she'll be all right."

Jodie looked up at the judges. Tears were streaming down her cheeks — tears of pain and shame and bewilderment. "I can't go on," she sobbed. "I just can't."

The judges nodded, and the announcer boomed out her final humiliation. "Withdrawn. Number 14 — Monarch, ridden by Jodie Carpenter — has withdrawn. Bad luck. The next competitor is Lindy Smith on Quickfire, followed by Amanda Ritchie on Superior."

Old Bert Martin took the cigarette out of his mouth with his yellow fingers and watched Jodie limp away. "Yeah, bad luck for the little Carpenter girl." He studied her retreat. "Blooming horses, you never know what they're going to do. Go like the breeze one day and buck like broncos the next."

When Tanya had caught Monarch, she calmed him down and walked him back to the trailer. Jodie hobbled over and rubbed her tear-stained face against his neck. "It wasn't your fault," she said over and over. "It wasn't your fault at all."

Her father tried to cheer her up. "Never mind, love. You win some and you lose some."

Alan joined in too. "Sure. You'll be a world beater next year."

They couldn't know that Jodie would never ride a horse again.

5

WHEN THEY ARRIVED home, her mother put Jodie straight to bed and telephoned the clinic. Saturday evening was an awkward time and Dr. Manners was busy, but his wife said he would come as soon as he could. He arrived an hour or two later but he didn't really help. Jodie was sure he was looking for clues in the wrong places.

"So you had a fall today?" he said, as if to suggest that the fall had caused the pain, instead of the other way around. "Luckily nothing is broken."

"It's not that," Jodie answered desperately. "It's my hands and hips and knees." But he seemed to think she was exaggerating.

After he had left the room, she heard him talking to her parents on the verandah. "Keep her warm," he said. "She's suffering a certain amount of shock. Bruising too, and some swelling. Here's a prescription. Try to get the pills from the night pharmacy. They'll calm her down a bit and help her to get a good night's sleep."

Jodie turned her face to the wall and sobbed. The pain was brutal. No matter how she lay in bed it went on unchanged. And the day's disaster rankled in her heart just as painfully. Now everyone would be accusing her of poor riding. Oscar Hoffmann had virtually said so after the competition.

When the doctor had gone, she heard her father and mother talking in the kitchen. It almost developed into an argument.

"The doctor isn't getting to the bottom of it," her father said doggedly. "What's the use of pain-killers and sleeping pills?"

"I should think she needs them. She's had a fall."

"There's more to it than that."

"What?"

"I don't know. Perhaps it's hormones or something. Because she's growing up."

"Oh, for heaven's sake! She's still a little girl."

"Have you seen her hands? The knuckles are

35

swollen like walnuts. And her knee is puffed up as big as a rock melon."

"Well, she fell off a horse, remember?"

"It's got nothing to do with falling off a horse. It's internal. A sort of inflammation."

"From what?"

"How should I know?" he answered testily. "Maybe it's a virus."

"The doctor would have said so."

"The doctor doesn't know." He paused angrily. "But I'm going to find out. I'm not going to have her crying every day, getting about in agony, just because nobody knows what's wrong with her."

"What are you going to do?"

"Take her to a specialist. I'm going to ask old Bedside for a referral tomorrow."

It was not the kind of conversation that was likely to make Jodie feel any better. Even after her father had returned from the night pharmacy with her pills, she didn't sleep very well. She ached all over. The pain that had been like a separate string of fierce little fires in her knuckles and wrists and knees spread like a bushfire that raged over her whole body.

She didn't get up in the morning. Alan tried to cheer her by giving her breakfast in bed, but the effort of lifting a spoonful of cereal to her mouth was so diabolically painful that she gave up and just let her hands lie motionless on the bedspread. Even then they throbbed and ached so much that she had to keep moving them every minute or two in the blind hope that she could find a position that was less painful.

At lunchtime she got up laboriously and went to the bathroom for a shower. She was appalled at the look of her right knee — puffed up bigger than ever. It was impossible to put her weight on it, so she had to shuffle and hop, holding on to the doorknob and the taps and towel rack to keep her balance. The hot water was pleasantly soothing and she stayed under it for as long as she dared, fearful that she would drain the whole tank. Then she dressed slowly and hobbled out into the kitchen.

The others greeted her kindly. "No need for you to get up," her mother said. "Go back and snuggle under the blankets."

"I have to feed Monarch."

"You have to do no such thing. Alan fed him this morning, and Tanya is coming over this afternoon."

Jodie looked up in surprise. "Tanya is?"

"Yes. And she'll look after him until you're well again. She'll feed him, groom him, muck out his stable — everything. She phoned this morning."

Jodie was grateful. Although she was more particular and possessive about Monarch than about anything else in the world, she just didn't have the willpower at present to lift his heavy feed bin or push the wheelbarrow or do a dozen essential things in the stable. And if someone else had to do it for a while, who better than Tanya? She was a good rider, she was thorough and reliable, and she lived only half a mile away on the hill slope above Greenvale.

"Okay," Jodie said. "I'll have a talk to Tanya when she comes over this afternoon."

"In any case, you're going to spell him now, aren't you?"

"Yes, until the end of January."

"There you are. And by then you'll be as fit as a fiddle again."

Jodie didn't go to school on the following Monday or Tuesday. The pain was as bad as ever and she couldn't face all the pitying looks and sympathetic murmurs that were sure to be waiting for her after her fall in the Pony Club Cup — to say nothing of Amanda's gloating.

Luckily her father was working in Adelaide for the week, and so he was able to take her to the specialist — a Dr. Rodney Harper who, according to Dr. Manners, was "the best troubleshooter in town." His rooms were in a medical complex in North Adelaide — a vast warren of a place with doctors and nurses like white-coated rabbits darting in and out of their holes or hurrying down long corridors and disappearing in the distance.

Jodie's appointment was at two o'clock on Tuesday afternoon, but she and her father had to wait some time beyond that before being called in by Dr. Harper's nurse. Then there was another examination, a brief discussion of her sessions with Dr. Manners, and more questions about her recent activities. After that the nurse took some blood from a vein on the inside of Jodie's elbow. "Just a little pinprick," she said, pushing in the needle and drawing the blood up into the syringe. Jodie tried not to look at it, but it was hard to keep her gaze away.

A moment later Dr. Harper called someone on the telephone and she heard scraps of conversation with lots of strange words that she didn't understand. When he looked up he was both businesslike and kindly. "I'd like you to see another specialist now — Dr. Conrad Klein. He's here in this building. The nurse will show you the way."

Off yet again went Jodie and her father, down another corridor and into another burrow. The nurse knocked and opened the door. "Doctor, this is Mr. Carpenter and his daughter, Jodie," she announced.

Dr. Klein was a military-looking man with a small clipped beard. He seemed to know a great deal about Jodie without ever having seen her before. After a short discussion he asked her to sit up on a couch while he examined her fingers, wrists, and knees with great care. His hands were quick and sensitive, like the hands of a musician.

"I'm going to take some fluid from that knee, Jodie," he said. Then, with just the hint of a smile, he added, "You won't mind parting with it, I'm sure."

Although she tried not to show it, she was frightened when he began to break the seal on a sterilized parcel containing bowls, swabs, syringes, and bandages. He swabbed the knee with iodine, using a pair of tweezers and cotton wool. "Not allergic to iodine, are you?" he asked.

"I don't know. I don't think so."

He made a mark like a tiny cross on her knee, almost like the cross wires in a gun sight. She was uneasy at the thought that he was going to use her knee for target practice. Finally he took up the syringe and filled it with anaesthetic from a small narrow bottle. "Just a little pinprick," he said. She was beginning to hate those words.

The needle went in deeper and deeper, and a strangely unreal feeling spread from it, as if her knee no longer belonged to her. When he had driven in the needle so far that Jodie felt sure that the point was about to come out on the other side, he deftly unscrewed the syringe, leaving the needle embedded in her knee. A moment later he screwed on a tiny suction pump and pulled up the plunger very slowly and carefully. As it rose, the cylinder below it began to fill with distasteful-looking liquid, like dirty pineapple juice.

Jodie watched, fascinated. She couldn't quite believe that it was coming from her own body. When he had filled the little cylinder he squirted the fluid into a phial and stuck a tag on it. After that he repeated the process several more times until her knee seemed to have been drained completely and the suction pump began to slurp air and bubbles. He then replaced the pump with another syringe and injected a drug of some kind into her knee before withdrawing the needle altogether. The puncture didn't even bleed.

"Right, Jodie, you can stand up now," he said.

She did so gingerly, expecting the searing pain to return.

"Does that feel better?"

"I can't believe it," she answered. "It doesn't hurt at all."

He smiled. "For the moment."

She was downcast. "D'you mean the pain'll come back again?"

He nodded. "I'm afraid it will, Jodie."

She looked him in the eye. "What's the matter with me, then?"

He paused, eyeing her sadly. "You have a disease, Jodie."

She was suddenly very frightened. "What . . . what sort of disease?"

"It's called arthritis."

Jodie's father started in amazement. "Arthritis? At *her* age?"

Dr. Klein nodded again. "And I'm afraid it's rheumatoid arthritis, one of the worst forms."

Jodie's father looked at him in bewilderment. "But arthritis is for old people, surely?"

Dr. Klein shook his head. "Not juvenile arthritis. It strikes young people at all ages: teenagers, children, toddlers, even babies. Believe me, I've seen them all."

Jodie was still frightened. "How did I get it? What causes it?"

He smiled wanly. "If I knew that, I'd be the happiest person in the world."

"Don't you know?"

"Nobody really knows. Not yet."

"Can't you cure it, then?"

"Maybe not *cure*. But we can help. We can help a lot."

He filled out a form on his desk and handed it to Jodie. "Take this form to the office at the end of the corridor and they'll show you what to do. I want you to have some X rays. When you've finished, you can join your father back in the waiting room."

She wondered whether he was just trying to get rid of her. The two men watched her go out. "I still can't believe it," Jodie's father said. "Arthritis? In a healthy young girl?"

"It doesn't respect anyone, Mr. Carpenter."

"But she can be treated for it?"

"Certainly. As I've said, we can do a lot for her."

"But not enough?"

"Probably not enough."

"She could get worse?"

"She could."

Dr. Klein shuffled some papers and wrote some

notes on a medical card. "I want to see Jodie again next week," he said. "By then we'll have all the results of X rays, blood tests, and so on. Then we'll be able to work out the best treatment for her. In the meantime, I'll prescribe some pills to try to ease the inflammation."

Jodie's father left the office and walked slowly down to the waiting room. He felt that a dark shadow had suddenly blotted the sunshine from Jodie's life—and from his own.

6

WHEN JODIE and her father returned to Dr. Klein the following week, he was actually waiting for them. A set of big X rays lay on his desk when they entered, and he immediately took these and began putting them up on the wall in front of a special light screen that looked like hard white glass.

Jodie had never had an X ray before, and it made her feel uncomfortable to think that people were peering at parts of her like this, as if she'd been undressed right down to her skeleton. But Dr. Klein was quite matter-of-fact about it all. "This is your right knee, Jodie," he said energetically, "and this one over here is the left."

Jodie and her father both stared, but said nothing.

"You can see that already there's a lot of damage to the cartilage. It's almost nonexistent in places"—he pointed with his finger—"here and here." He kept popping up more pictures. "Here are Jodie's hips, which aren't good either. This is her left hand, and this one is the right. They're both in very bad shape."

Watching him and listening to his gloomy comments, Jodie almost began to feel guilty, as if she had just taken an important exam and failed. Far in the back of her mind she could hear Mr. Harrison putting her down: "Look at this page, Jodie! It really is very poor. And this one here is terrible. As for that assignment there, it's one of the worst I've seen."

When Dr. Klein had finished his X-ray picture show, he told her that the tests on her blood also showed that the disease was rampant in her body. By that time Jodie and her father were both so depressed that they felt like crying.

Her father cleared his throat. "What now?"

"Treatment. Regular treatment."

"What sort of treatment?"

"We'll start with gold."

Jodie couldn't believe her ears. "Did you say *gold*?"

"Yes, gold injections." He saw the expression on her face and smiled. "Don't worry. You won't turn into a gold mine."

"I hope not," Jodie's father said, trying to be cheerful. "I couldn't afford it."

As always, Dr. Klein was businesslike. "She will have to have a good many doses. I'll prepare the prescriptions, but I'll arrange for you to have the injections at your own clinic so that you don't have to come all the way to the city every time."

That was the beginning of Jodie's never-ending treatment. Every week or so she had to visit Dr. Manners, who filled a syringe from a tiny bottle full of golden liquid that he injected into her arm. She disliked the injections. They hurt for some time afterward, and they didn't seem to do her any good.

Christmas came and went but it was not a happy time for Jodie, in spite of gifts and cards and a lovely Christmas dinner. For by now it was plain that she was going to be handicapped for a long time—perhaps forever. She found it painful to walk, painful to stand, painful to lie in bed. She had little strength in her hands and legs. Many of the simple tasks of everyday life, like combing her hair or brushing her teeth, were almost beyond her. She couldn't bend her fingers or lift up her arms far enough. As part of her treatment she also had to take pills—ten of them every day. There were white pills, red pills, yellow pills and green pills. Some looked like small white eyes or big round buttons. There were even cylindrical pills that looked like small electrical fuses. She disliked them all.

There was worse to come. Early in the new year an ulcer formed on the inside of her arm, just below the elbow. It was as big as a fifty-cent piece, and it was ugly and painful. After a few days the skin broke and it became a weeping sore. Jodie couldn't bear to have anything touching or rubbing against it, not even the flimsiest of blouses, so she wore shirts with short sleeves. Although that was easy to do in the summer months, she dreaded the onset of winter.

The ulcer on her arm had scarcely begun to heal when another one broke out on her shoulder, followed by one on her thigh and another behind her left knee. They were deep and horrible, and they made walking more difficult than ever. Jodie's mother spent a long time each morning trying to dress them lightly with bandages of thin gauze, but the slightest pressure made them unbearable. And no sooner had one started to improve than several more appeared elsewhere.

After a week or two Jodie's father took her back

48

to Dr. Klein. At first he and several other specialists were inclined to think that the ulcers had nothing to do with her arthritis, and it was only when Jodie's father couldn't bear to watch her struggling and wincing anymore that he stormed back and demanded that something be done. "She didn't have ulcers until she started taking those damned pills," he shouted. "Her skin was perfect before that."

Dr. Klein was patient and cooperative, as he always was. "Very well," he answered, "we'll take her off some of the pills. But she may have a bad flareup within a day or two. You'll have to be prepared for that."

Whether Jodie's father was right or wrong, the ulcers slowly subsided after that. They left nasty scars on her skin, but luckily none had broken out on her face.

There were also human problems. If Jodie told people that she couldn't do certain things because of her arthritis, they didn't believe her. Some of the boys at school laughed at the idea. "Pull my other leg," they'd say. "Arthritis? You have to be joking."

At home things were difficult too. She couldn't do anything quickly anymore, so she slowed up the household routine when everyone was in a hurry. She couldn't move fast, couldn't snatch things up or fling them down. One morning, when she was struggling to get a carton of milk and a dishful of eggs from the fridge, she dropped the dish. There was nothing careless about it. The dish simply fell from her hand because she couldn't grip it tightly enough. The results were calamitous. Half a dozen eggs disintegrated on the kitchen floor in a dreadful ruin of broken shells, slippery whites, and oozing yellow yolk.

"Jodie," her mother exploded. "For heaven's sake, look what you've done!"

Jodie flushed and tried to scrape some of the mess into a dustpan, but she couldn't bend down far enough and her hands hurt terribly when she gripped the handle of the scraper.

"Here, let me," her mother said brusquely, kneeling on the floor with a dishcloth. "Just get out of the way. We're late already."

It was a bad moment for both of them. Jodie felt hurt and her mother quickly felt guilty. But it was just another example, one of hundreds, that showed how people failed to understand Jodie's handicap. She was not regarded as sick, but rather as clumsy, inept, slow, incapable. In short, as something of a nuisance.

At her new school it was worse. Some people there even thought she was a fraud, a malingerer, who was trading on a few aches and pains to win sympathy. "Laying it on a bit thick, ain't she?" she heard Angus McPherson say one day. "Is she trying to suck up to the teachers or something?" Jodie's cheeks burned as she hobbled away. She wished that just once, for five minutes, she could transfer the pain from her own body to Angus McPherson's. Then perhaps he would understand.

Early in April Grandma Hooper—her mother's mother, who lived in Victoria—came to stay for a month's holiday. She was a wizened little woman with a beaked nose, a frizz of white hair, beady eyes, and a tireless tongue. She thought she knew almost everything there was to know about everything, but most of all she was an expert on illnesses. No matter what the malady was, Gran had virtually died of it—"I was as good as dead," she always said—or her neighbor had died of it, or her neighbor's daughter's friend's teenage son was about to die of it. She knew all about pneumonia, pleurisy, angina, and tetanus. She was on close terms with measles, whooping cough, kidney disease, and high blood pressure. Her body had battled mightily with gallstones, shingles, dyspepsia, and chronic stomach cramps. But of all the illnesses in medical history, the one she thought she knew most about was arthritis.

51

"Good grief, child," she said to Jodie as soon as she arrived. "You shouldn't have arthritis at your age. What on earth have they been feeding you?"

For a moment Jodie was bewildered. "Feeding me?"

"Yes, child, yes. What have they been giving you to eat?"

Jodie's mother answered for her. "She eats whatever we do."

"Hah! And at school?"

Jodie started to open her mouth, but she didn't get a chance to reply.

"Pastry, I'll bet. Pie, cake, sugar, potato chips, sausage rolls. Junk food."

"Well . . ."

"No wonder you've got arthritis. It's caused by food, you know. By diet."

Jodie's mother tried to interrupt. "Her specialist says it's a disease. He has put her on a lot of pills."

Granny Hooper threw up her arms. "Pills! Pills are the worst thing you can take for arthritis. They poison the system."

"I should think the doctors ought to know what they're doing."

"Doctors don't know anything. I've proved that

a dozen times. No, no. Tomorrow, Helen, we'll go down to town and bring back some proper food for the girl. We'll have her right in no time. I had arthritis in my back once. The doctors gave me up. They said I was the worst case they'd ever seen. But now I'm as fit as a fiddle again. Cured myself."

"By eating?" Jodie's father asked. There was just a hint of mockery in his voice.

Granny shot him a suspicious glance. "Yes." And with that she marched out of the room.

"Blooming old blowhard," he muttered under his breath. "She's a windbag and a hypochondriac."

Jodie didn't know what a hypochondriac was but it sounded unpleasant.

For the next month Jodie wasn't allowed to eat anything unless Granny approved of it. She couldn't have sugar, sweets, Coke, or cake. Red meat was banned too, and so were nuts, lemon juice, white bread, ice cream, pastry, buns, and biscuits. Fish and chicken were the only meats allowed. For most of the time she had to live on lettuce, carrots, beans, and celery. After three days she was fed up. "I'm starting to feel like a rabbit," she said.

Alan smirked. "You hop like one."

She tried to throw a dish towel at him, but it hurt her shoulder so much that she winced.

In addition to supplying Jodie with loads of rabbit food, Granny also brought back books for her to read — paperback books about arthritis. There were lots of pictures in them of skeletons with deformed bones, photographs of twisted hands and fingers, and diagrams of joints without cartilage. And of course there were dozens of sure-fire remedies. Because Jodie had to stay inside so much, she had plenty of time to look through them. She soon realized that the writers often disagreed with one another, and so she started to needle Granny by reading contradictory passages.

"It says in this book that tomatoes are very bad for people with arthritis. They've got too much acid."

Granny came in with a rush. "Of course they're bad for you. They're the worst thing you can possibly eat. They belong to the deadly nightshade family — real poison."

Jodie held up another book, trying to look innocent. "But this book says tomatoes are very good for you. They should be part of every salad."

"Huh, that fellow's a fool. He doesn't know what he's talking about."

"It's a woman, actually."

"Well, she ought to know better."

Sometimes Alan also skimmed through a chapter or two and joined in the game. "No wonder we can't get rid of arthritis in this country," he said when they were all having morning tea one Sunday.

Everyone looked up inquisitively, especially Granny. "Why?"

Alan turned a couple of pages in the book he was holding up. "There's an old Russian recipe here. It says you should bury yourself up to the neck in warm camel dung twice a week." He looked up with a wickedly innocent face. "We just haven't got enough camels."

Jodie's father almost choked on his biscuit, but Granny was furious at such vulgar talk. She sat up straight with a stony expression. "That was in the olden days, for primitive people."

"But if it worked for them it should work for us," Alan said. "Perhaps horse dung would do. Maybe Monarch could help." He and his father couldn't hold back their mirth any longer, and their shoulders began to shake with silent laughter.

Granny was disgusted. "Mock as much as you like. That's the trouble with you people these days. You're all smart-alecks. You don't believe in anything anymore. No faith."

"But it's hard when you don't know what to believe." Alan held up a third book. "In here there's a list of all the things you should eat if you want to be cured, but they only grow in Burma and Thailand—black beans, herbs, bark, peel, a special kind of seed . . . all in southeast Asia. Nowhere else."

Gran was defensive. "There's nothing wrong with that."

"No, but it makes you wonder. Wouldn't you think God would have let a few good things grow in other parts of the world too—in Europe or Africa or America, even in Australia?"

Granny stood up haughtily. "Poor Jodie will never get better, I can see that," she said loudly. "Not in this house."

7

EVERY AFTERNOON Jodie dragged herself down to the stables as best she could to talk to Tanya and to watch her working Monarch. She always took down a cube of sugar for him and they played a game while he searched for it, nosing and nuzzling about until she revealed it in her cupped hand. They were still as close, Jodie and her horse, as they had ever been. Nevertheless it was a cruel and confusing time for her. She was grateful to have someone like Tanya coming over every day—her helper and very best friend—but it broke her heart not to be able to ride Monarch herself.

At first the arrangement was regarded as just a temporary measure. Tanya was to help out for a while until Jodie was able to take over again. But the days dragged into weeks, and the weeks into months, with no sign of improvement. In fact things were getting steadily worse. Her knee kept on swelling and had to be drained every so often. Her right leg began to twist at an angle, giving her a knock-kneed look. From time to time her knees or hips or ankles had to be given deep injections of cortisone. The knuckles on her hands were permanently swollen into big lumps, with hideously painful nodules that were always red and inflamed. And her wrists and shoulders burned cruelly at the slightest movement. Although the new show-jumping season was in full swing again, it was obvious that she couldn't ride in any of the competitions. There was no hope of that. None whatever.

One Sunday afternoon after she had spent an hour watching Tanya and Monarch in the menage, she struggled back to the house and went straight to her room. She had some homework to finish for Mrs. Stone, her English teacher at Hillbank High School. It was due the following morning, and Mrs. Stone was not the sort of person who made allowances, not even for people handicapped because of asthma, broken legs, or arthritis.

Jodie spread her books all around her, found a clean sheet of paper, and took up her "palm pen" — a plastic ball slightly bigger than a Ping-Pong ball with a ballpoint pen driven through the middle of it. She was able to hold it quite well and write with much less pain because she didn't have to bend her fingers nearly as much, or press as tightly as she had to with an ordinary pen or pencil. It was one of a dozen clever ideas that her father had brought back from the Arthritis Foundation in Adelaide — gadgets to turn taps, pull out drawers, open bottles and jars, pick up pins — that helped to make life a little easier for people with crippled joints.

She had been working silently for about half an hour when her mother and father walked into the kitchen next door to her room to make a cup of tea. They had been talking, and they obviously thought she was still out in the menage with Tanya.

"We'll have to make a decision soon," her mother said. "We can't let things go on as they are. It's not fair to anybody."

Her father was silent. It seemed as if he couldn't bring himself to say anything.

"When decisions have to be made," she went on, "it's better to make them and get it over with."

"Making a decision is easy," he answered at last. "But making the right decision is very hard."

"Well, she's not going to be able to ride again, is she? That's quite obvious. So what's the use of a horse if she can't ride it?"

A tingle of dread swept over Jodie. They were talking about *her*. And about Monarch.

Her father spoke sadly. "What would it do to Jodie?"

"She'd get used to it."

"She wouldn't, you know. It isn't a rabbit or cockatoo you're talking about. It's a horse."

"A horse is no different from anything else."

"Oh yes it is. She loves that horse. She talks to it like a human being. As she says, it's a soul mate."

"Good God, you're getting as bad as she is."

Jodie sat in her room scarcely daring to breathe —gripping her palm pen so rigidly that, in spite of the pain, she was in danger of crushing the ball.

There was a long pause. "She'd lose hope," her father said at last. "She'd stop fighting and give up. It's the one thing that keeps her going."

"But there's no point to it. She's going to be handicapped for the rest of her life."

"That's just why we have to be so careful."

Jodie's mother was getting impatient. "For heaven's sake, Ben, what's the point of keeping a horse for her now? Are we just going to let things drag on until Monarch drops dead from old age?"

"That could be part of the treatment."

"Rubbish. Look, he's a good horse now but he won't be worth a cabbage in ten years' time. He'll be too old. We'd get a good price for him if we sold him tomorrow. And it would help to pay some of her bills."

"Shh," he answered uneasily. "She might hear you."

Jodie had heard right enough — every word. Her breathing was fast and feverish. She couldn't believe her ears. They were planning to sell Monarch. Sell him, and use the money to pay for X rays or blood tests or rotten lousy pills.

"No," she yelled, pushing herself up from her desk and hobbling desperately to the door. She flung it open and stood there wide-eyed, holding on to the door frame. "You're not selling Monarch."

Her mother and father were taken completely by surprise. They tried to calm her. "Look, love, we were just talking about—"

"You're not selling him. You're not. He's mine, he's mine. . . ." Her small body looked smaller than ever, her face white, her dark eyes bright with fear and anger.

"Now, Jodie, don't get yourself—"

Her mother cut in impatiently. "We have to be practical, dear."

"You're not selling him." It was a yell, a defiant shout.

"Just try to be a bit reasonable while we—"

"If you try to sell him I'll take him away."

"Oh, for goodness' sake, Jodie, be sensible."

"No." Jodie was screaming, on the verge of hysteria. "No, no, no."

Her father came forward quickly and took her by the shoulders. "Now, now," he said gently. "You know we wouldn't do anything without talking it over with you first."

She buried her face against his jacket and burst into an uncontrollable storm of sobbing. She was like a little girl again. "Please," she cried. "Please, Daddy. Don't sell Monarch."

He pressed her shoulders reassuringly. "There, there. Calm down now, and don't worry."

That night she was feverish, and by the following morning the disease had flared up so much that it seemed to be ravaging every bone in her body. Her father was due to leave for Broken Hill, but he was so worried about her that he telephoned his office and arranged to take a week's leave. Then he contacted Dr. Klein urgently and managed to get an appointment with him just before lunch. The doctor examined Jodie again and took more blood samples.

While she was still in the consulting room, he took her father aside for a quick word. "She's in the middle of a big flareup," he said. "I'm afraid she's in for a bad time. I'm going to arrange for her to have a few weeks in the hospital."

"In the hospital?"

"Yes, in the rheumatology ward. We'll try to stabilize her condition. When she comes home again, try to help her as much as you can."

"In what way?"

"Encourage her to cope, but don't molly-coddle her. She has to try to stand on her own two feet, if that's not an unfortunate way of putting it."

Jodie's father was thoughtful. "Doctor, d'you think anxiety affects people with arthritis?" he asked. "You know — fear, worry, stress?"

"It isn't easy to be sure about that. But anything that worsens a person's health is bad."

"D'you think people tend to give up when they're worried?"

"Yes, they're more vulnerable." He paused. "Why? Is Jodie worried about something?"

Jodie's father took a deep breath. "She has a horse . . ." he began. And so it all came out.

Dr. Klein was very interested. "In that case don't sell the horse. Hang on to it if you possibly can. At the moment we certainly don't want to complicate things even more for Jodie. She has enough to cope with as it is. She badly needs something to brighten her up and give her a lift."

If Jodie had been able to overhear what Dr. Klein was saying, her spirits would have lifted without a doubt.

8

JODIE WAS ADMITTED to the hospital at three o'clock on the following Thursday afternoon. The place terrified her. It was so huge, so crowded with people, that she felt as insignificant as an ant in the tunnels of Gibraltar.

People were hurrying everywhere, but nobody was interested in her. Doctors were hastening this way and that in white coats with little photographs of themselves pinned to their lapels. Great gaggles of nurses were coming off duty or going on duty, talking, laughing and waving their hands — all engrossed in their own concerns. Orderlies were pushing beds down seemingly endless corridors or maneuvering them into elevators; technicians were making for unknown destinations with tool kits and screwdrivers; patients were lining up for blood tests or X rays; florists' messengers were bustling past with bowls of blooms that were meant to lighten someone's misery in a hidden corner of this vast concrete anthill.

Jodie and her mother had to wait until the staff had time to take down all her details and assign her to a bed. There were no spare chairs. "You'd think that in a place concerned with handicapped people they'd at least have somewhere for you to sit," her mother said waspishly.

The pain in Jodie's ankles, knees, and hips was so bad that by the time her particulars had been punched into a computer, she could barely drag herself to the elevator in the wake of Nurse Bolton, who was leading the way up to the rheumatology ward.

"If you're not a hospital case when you arrive, then you certainly are by the time they've finished with you," Jodie's mother growled. "They make sure of that." It was her attempt at black humor.

"Dr. Klein will be coming in to see you this evening," the nurse said to Jodie when they reached the ward. "He'll give you all the details of your treatment."

"What will that be?"

"Hydrotherapy every morning, I guess. Ray lamps, some physio and gentle exercise, finding what pills are best, and in what doses. For most of the time just rest." She bustled about, folding back the covers on the bed. "You may also have some practice using an electric wheelchair."

They both looked at her sharply. "Wheelchair?"

Nurse Bolton clearly felt she had gone too far, so she backpedaled hastily. "Oh, I don't really know. That's for Dr. Klein to say."

She helped Jodie into her pajamas and took her blood pressure, pulse, and weight. "Now, into bed," she said briskly. "You'd better get used to this place, because it's going to be your home for the next three weeks."

Jodie crawled under the blankets. She looked so tiny in the high white bed — like a hurt animal cringing in a burrow — that her mother felt a sudden catch in her throat. She pressed Jodie's hand. "I have to go now," she said softly, "but I'll come in to visit you every day, and so will Dad and Alan whenever they can. And Mr. and Mrs. Thompson will be coming in sometimes with Tanya. She'll be able to tell you all about Monarch — how he's doing." She kissed Jodie. " 'Bye, love. Dr. Klein and the nurses will look after you. They really will." She pressed Jodie's hand again and made for the door.

Jodie didn't say anything. She turned her face toward the harsh bare whiteness of the hospital wall. A big tear welled from her eye and slid slowly down her cheek onto the pillow.

For the next three weeks Jodie ceased to be an independent human being. She was a number, a statistic, a name on a medical chart. To the doctors and nurses who came into her room in cycles she was a bulge in the bed, a crooked body that had just replaced a similar body, that in turn had replaced the one before that. Most of them had to peer at her chart in order to find out what her name was, and even then some of them got it wrong, turning Jodie into Jackie or Jade or even Tobie.

Her mother and Dr. Klein were the only stable points in her existence. They came every day and kept her in touch with reality — her mother with news of home and school and the antics of the outside world, and Dr. Klein with talk of tests and pills, side effects and subtle changes in her illness.

There were dreary daily routines repeated as regularly as the movements of machines: the taking of temperature and the testing of blood pressure, the making of beds and the washing of bodies, the swallowing of pills and the answering of questions about bowels and bladders. From time to time there were also more jabbings with needles and more suckings up of blood into syringes, and occasionally more X rays of nodular knuckles and puffed-up knees.

Meals were monotonous too, although the staff tried hard to make them interesting. But Jodie was seldom hungry, and she disliked having to eat in bed. At the best of times it was hard for her to handle a knife and fork with her deformed fingers, or to lift a cup to her lips while shafts of pain were lancing through her wrists. To do it in bed, when every painful movement was likely to cause a catastrophe all over the white bedspread, was an endless torment. And spooning soup up into her mouth was simply impossible.

Her hydrotherapy session in the warm pool was the happiest part of the day. Although an orderly took her down to the ground floor in a wheelchair, she was able to put on her swimsuit by herself, slowly and painfully, and even get into the pool on her own. After that she was given exercises in the water by a specially trained nurse, and then she was allowed to have some time in the pool by herself. She liked this most of all—just to lie there like a basking fish beside the handrail, with the water buoying up her body and the warmth easing the fiendish pain in her joints.

Unhappily, the session had to end, no matter how much she tried to prolong it. And once she was out of the pool, it didn't take long for the agonies to return—the wolves of pain, as Dr. Klein called them, snapping and biting, sinking their fangs into her legs and arms.

In spite of everything, after a couple of weeks Dr. Klein began to be more hopeful. He was pleased with her progress. He said that she had been through a most fearful flareup but there were signs that it was easing. He called it a "period of remission." He was hoping to stabilize the disease for a few years until she was old enough to have surgery. Then they might be able to replace some of her rotten joints with ones made of stainless steel and plastic, which would do away with most of the pain. In the meantime he said she should use a wheelchair as much as possible—a light electric one that would fold up and fit into the trunk of a car—to ease the load on her bones and slow down the rate of damage.

At last, after almost four weeks, she was allowed to go back home. That night, in her own bed in her own precious room, she cried with relief. The disease was still with her, and it always would be, but she felt more confident in her own surroundings. And she was near Monarch again. In the days that followed, she was able to trundle down to the stables in the wheelchair her father bought and reach up to pat Monarch's nose as she always had. And he in turn bent forward with his graceful neck and nudged her cheek, looking for the sugar cube he knew she had brought for him. His touch was the best homecoming present she could have wished for.

Even though everyone had agreed that Monarch would never be sold, things were not easy for Jodie. For a start there had to be a proper arrangement with Tanya, so the two families — the Thompsons and the Carpenters — sat down for an earnest discussion over tea and scones one Sunday morning. Jodie had the final say in every decision.

It was agreed that Monarch would stay in his own stable and his own paddock, but that Tanya would do all the training and ride him in all the shows. Mr. Thompson insisted on paying half the monthly feed bill, and Jodie's father said that Tanya could borrow the horse trailer whenever she liked, because it was better for it to be traveling about

71

on the road than standing in the shed and slowly rusting away. Tanya, of course, had to pay the entrance fee for every event she contested, and she also had to pay the blacksmith whenever Monarch needed a new set of shoes. Either Jodie or Tanya could break off the agreement at any time if things didn't work out.

Tanya was beside herself with joy. She had never been able to afford a horse of her own, and now she had the use of one of the best jumpers in the district. Three weeks later she signed up for her first real test. Naturally, Jodie and her parents went along too and watched eagerly from the sidelines. Sitting in her wheelchair near the boundary rail of the arena, Jodie was almost as nervous as she would have been if she had been competing. Luckily Tanya seemed to cope very well, even though Monarch minced and snorted because he hadn't been in a competition for so long. He also had to get used to Tanya's style. She was much bigger than Jodie, and she tended to sit more heavily in the saddle.

They had purposely chosen a small meet at Gum Flat, where there were lower jumps and fewer spectators. It was wise to give Tanya a bit of experience in places like that before asking her to tackle the tough rivalry of the bigger shows. She did well, despite a few heart-stopping moments at the second combination, where Monarch pranced and craw-fished as he came up. For a second it looked as though he might refuse.

"Straighten him up, straighten him up," Jodie said under her breath. "Come on, Monarch. You can do it."

The Thompsons and Carpenters were all sitting together, gazing at Tanya intently. "I can't bear to watch," Mrs. Thompson said. She seemed to have taken over that saying from Jodie's mother.

Luckily, Monarch found his rhythm just in time and went clear. In the jump-off against the clock, a little later on, he pulled a rail but still managed to scrape into second place.

When the ribbons were being awarded, the announcer had all the facts right: "The second place getter is Monarch, owned by Jodie Carpenter and ridden by Tanya Thompson. And what a beautiful little horse he is, too." Jodie didn't know until years later that her father had made sure her name was included in the announcement.

As soon as the ceremony was over, Tanya rode across to Jodie. The red ribbon around Monarch's neck shone in the sunlight. Tanya took off her riding helmet and let her blond hair blow loose in the breeze. She was beaming with delight.

Jodie used the arms of her chair to push herself up and let Monarch nuzzle her hand. "Good boy," she said. "Very good boy." She had his cube of sugar ready for him, and he gobbled it up eagerly.

Tanya leaned forward from the saddle and patted him on the neck for the twentieth time. "Wasn't he fantastic?" she said. Then, seeing the look of longing and loss in Jodie's face, she added hastily, "Of course, if *you'd* been riding him, he would have come first."

A great sob welled up in Jodie's throat and she turned away quickly to hide the tears in her eyes. She knew that from now on every weekend was going to be like this, with Tanya Thompson the focus of everyone's gaze in the center of the arena, but with Jodie Carpenter in a wheelchair, eating her heart out beyond the boundary fence.

Slowly and relentlessly the disease made Jodie's limbs more deformed. Her fingers were getting as crooked as claws and her knees were bent like an old man's. She remained very small, her growth stunted. Once a month she went down to Adelaide with her mother or father to see Dr. Klein and various other specialists. They assured her that surgery would eventually help her, but that it could be done only when she had stopped growing. Jodie

74

shrugged and smiled wryly. "I thought I'd stopped growing long ago," she said.

Dr. Klein shook his head. "Oh no. Not until you're sixteen or seventeen at least. You can imagine what would happen if we put in an artificial joint and your body kept on growing afterward."

At home Jodie's mother was not impressed. "That's all very well," she said, "but what does Jodie do in the meantime?"

She was right, of course. There was not a moment of the day when Jodie was free of pain. She often wondered how her body could possibly have so many places that hurt, and in so many different ways. There were broad lakes of pain like pools of acid lying under the skin, spears of pain, throbbing points worse than the worst toothache in the world, and patches as fierce as fire—burns that no treatment could soothe. Sometimes, especially when the pain came in shafts like white-hot skewers hammered into the bone, she found it hard to think of anything else. She couldn't sleep at night or concentrate during the day.

Her schoolwork suffered, not only because she missed so many days but because she was often so doped up with painkillers that her head felt full of cotton wool and the world looked furry around the edges.

75

Meanwhile Granny Hooper kept up her flow of miracle cures from her home in Victoria. Every second mail brought a parcel or packet with detailed instructions. One week it was a jar of Epsom salts: "Take as much as you can heap on a five-cent piece, in warm water, every morning before breakfast. It'll clear the poisons out of your system."

Alan laughed hilariously when he read it. "Yes, and it'll clear out everything else as well."

The next week it was a hank of sweet-corn hair: "Boil this up, strain it, and drink the water before going to bed." Then it was cod liver oil mixed with orange juice, or prunes soaked in gin, or special herbs from Bangkok, canned shellfish from New Zealand, aloe vera, royal jelly, and an ointment made from a secret formula of goanna oil and ground fish scales.

Alan called it quackery and scoffed wholeheartedly. "Tell you what, sis," he said to Jodie. "I'm going to write a book and make a fortune telling people how to cure their arthritis."

She looked up and smiled wearily. "How?"

"With my new miracle magic method."

"What's that?"

"Hang a dead sea horse around your neck, put a copper bangle through your nose, and wear a string of macadamia nuts around your wrist."

She laughed outright. "Go away, you ass."

"If you can't get macadamias, then anything nutty will do."

She laughed even more. She liked Alan and his outrageous ways. Perhaps, after all, his light-hearted nonsense was the best treatment she could have.

9

SOMETIMES there were serious suggestions about new treatments for Jodie, which experts like Dr. Klein supported. One of these was acupuncture.

"Give it a try," he said when Jodie's father asked some questions about it one day. "Anything reasonable is worth a try."

"But will it do any good?"

"It won't cure Jodie. But it may give her some relief."

Arrangements were therefore made for Jodie to pay a series of visits to Dr. Wu Fung Cheng. Her mother drove her down to town and sat in the waiting room while Jodie had her first treatment.

Dr. Wu was a Chinese specialist who had come to Australia from Vietnam, and everyone said he was the best person to go to. He was a small man with round cheeks, slightly graying hair, and oval glasses. He wore a full-length white coat over his clothes, like a medical orderly. Although he was still learning to speak English, Jodie could understand his questions and comments very well.

"Rheumatoid arthritis is bad," he said as he helped her up onto the couch. "Very bad disease. I sorry."

He was such a friendly, good-hearted man, and so genuinely concerned about his patients, that Jodie liked him at once. It was just as well that she did, because after giving her a thorough examination—her twentieth so far, she guessed—he brought out his needles. Jodie had never seen anything like them, even though by now she was quite used to seeing grisly instruments in hospitals and doctors' rooms. A wave of uneasiness swept over her, like the fear she had felt in the early days of her illness.

Dr. Wu was aware of it instantly. "You are afraid a little bit, no?"

"Yes."

"Yes, no?"

"A little bit."

He smiled understandingly. "You have not had acupuncture? Have not seen needles before?"

"No. They look awful."

They were wicked-looking things, twenty or more, with glistening points and strong shafts, some of them so long that Jodie was sure they could have been pushed through her body until the points came out on the other side.

"No need to frighten," Dr. Wu said reassuringly. "Needles not much hurt." He continued with his preparations.

"Really?" Jodie didn't sound at all convinced.

"But must know where to put. Must know how."

He read the look on Jodie's face and smiled again. "But you are not sure?"

She was trying to think of something to say that would not sound rude or doubting. "Well . . ."

He left the bench where he had been sterilizing his instruments and came over to her. His walk was quick and silent. It matched the fluid movements of his hands. "You not worry," he said. "In my country we have many exams with the needles. And for final exams, who is it we must practice the needles on?"

She shook her head. "I don't know."

He seemed to be enjoying a kind of private joke. "We must practice on our *professor*." He said the word loudly for emphasis. "And if we hurt him, we fail." His eyes were lively, as if he were reliving the drama of those days.

She grinned. "And you didn't hurt him?"

"I won prize!" He smiled delightedly again and then went back to his preparations. He had evidently decided that he had told Jodie quite enough of his own autobiography, but she was happy. She liked his little touches of warmth and humor.

"Now," he said, coming over with needles, bowls, swabs, and other paraphernalia. "We start."

She tensed up at once.

"Please," he said gently. "Not worry."

He began work on her right knee, explaining what he was going to do, and what she might expect. In spite of herself she found that she was fascinated by the way he pinpointed each place, by the way he seemed to fling the needle into it, by the way he then spun it rapidly as if trying to kindle a little fire under her skin. Almost immediately some kind of reaction took place deep in her flesh that she couldn't understand and couldn't even describe. Something was suddenly released down there, some strange floodgate was opened and a tiny river as fast and fluid as a tingle of electricity ran along some unknown channel in her body. Miraculously, Dr. Wu seemed to know when

81

it had happened. Each time he looked at her quickly and expectantly. "Is running?" he asked.

"Something's happening. It feels like a tingle deep down."

"Ahh."

"What is it, exactly?"

"Is running."

She wasn't sure whether he had misunderstood her question or whether he was choosing not to answer it.

When he had put five or six needles into her leg, he heated the shafts with a special sort of rod and spun them again. Once or twice there was a tiny twinge of pain as he did it, and again he seemed to know about it just as quickly as she did. "A bit strong?" he asked with a concerned note in his voice. "A little bit strong?"

"It's okay."

The treatment went on for some time, but at last he decided that Jodie had had enough for one day and began to remove the needles. He did it with a quick decisive flick — so fast that they were out before she realized it.

He smiled again. "Finish for today. More next time." He eyed her quizzically as he helped her down from the couch. "Was not bad?"

"No, fine. It wasn't bad at all."

She put her weight on her right leg as she stood up and was astonished to find that most of the pain had gone.

"A little bit better?" he asked.

"Yes, much better."

He seemed pleased. "Hands next time. Then arm, shoulder, neck."

On the way home her mother asked Jodie a lot of questions. She was suspicious of foreign medicine and she wanted to know exactly what had been going on. Jodie reassured her. Anything that took away some of the pain was welcome.

Unfortunately it was not a cure. As soon as she stopped having the treatment, the pain returned. Gradually the expense and the constant traveling week after week became too much of a burden for everyone and so they decided to put an end to it. On the day Jodie said good-bye to Dr. Wu, they were both sad. He was the nicest doctor she had ever known.

10

T HE TROUBLE with the world, Jodie decided, was that people knew either too much or too little. There were some like Dr. Klein who knew enough to fill a dozen books but who sometimes found it hard to explain things to her in simple language. And there were others like Granny Hooper who thought they knew all about her illness but didn't understand anything at all. Even some of the teachers at the school and the people in the town were like that. They came up to her and offered advice about arthritis. They did it with the very best of intentions, because they always seemed to have an aunt or a cousin or a friend from Crutches Creek who had cured herself completely.

"She was so crippled up," they'd say, "that she couldn't even put on her own dress or hold a cup of tea—and now she's playing golf and jogging every day."

"What was wrong with her?" Jodie usually asked.

"Arthritis, of course. She had it really bad."

"Yes, but what kind of arthritis?"

"What do you mean, 'what kind'?"

"There are nearly two hundred different kinds of arthritis."

"Good grief, are there? I didn't know that."

And so it would go on. What kind did Jodie have? Rheumatoid. Yes, they'd heard the word but thought it meant the same as rheumatism. Was it the one called The Crippler? What a horrible way of describing it. People shouldn't use words like that. Was there any hope of Jodie getting better? They certainly hoped so. Well, they had to be going. Shopping to do. " 'Bye, Jodie," they said, "see you soon."

She grew used to it after a while and answered politely unless someone tried to be funny at her expense. If any of the boys at school tried to be clever by asking her how Arthur Itis was, she told them he was a brother of Smart Aleck. Before long they respected her. Even Angus McPherson learned to button his lip. "Tell you what, Jodie Carpenter," he said one day, almost in admiration, "you sure haven't got arthritis in your tongue."

Strangely, that was the beginning of a genuine friendship with Angus. Two things helped to cement it — her wheelchair and a brace on her left leg. The brace was Dr. Klein's idea after a new set of X rays showed that Jodie's ankle was deteriorating badly. It was a simple shaft of metal that swiveled in a bracket through the heel of her shoe and ran up beside her calf to a padded strap around her leg below the knee. Dr. Klein hoped that by transferring some of the load farther up the leg, the brace might protect the ankle and ease the pain in it. Jodie wasn't so sure. She suspected that they were merely switching the problem from one spot to another.

But the brace had a very different and unexpected benefit. As soon as she started wearing it, people's attitudes changed. They were much more attentive and sympathetic, because now they could actually see something of her problem. It was as if she at last had something to show for it, something to prove her handicap, to show that it was real. And so it was with Angus. He started carrying her books from lesson to lesson for her, helped her undo bottle tops and the lids of stubborn jars in the science laboratory, even opened doors for her. It was done quite naturally, without fuss or bravado. She began to see things she hadn't noticed before — that he was kind, reliable, and good-looking, with merry eyes and a shock of unruly brown hair.

Meanwhile Jodie found that she could no longer travel on the school bus. Quite apart from the problem of getting up and down the steep steps there was the hassle of folding up the wheelchair and finding a spot for it. Her mother therefore decided to drive her in the station wagon. She rearranged her own day so that she could drop Jodie and the chair at Hillbank High School on her way to work in the morning, and pick her up again after school. On most mornings Angus and Tanya or Lynn were waiting at the gate to help unload. Once Jodie was in the chair, she could manage very well by herself by operating the switches — forward and reverse — on the electric motor, although someone often gave her an extra push up the ramp to save power so that the batteries wouldn't run down during the day.

She became an expert with the chair, wheeling smoothly around corners, dashing into classrooms, stopping short within a half inch of tables or benches. In the long corridors that ran down the wings and the central block of the school she could develop quite a turn of speed. The vinyl floors were so highly polished that there was little friction, and the lightweight chair gathered astonishing momentum. She became Jodie Carpenter, ace of the Formula One Wheelchair Grand Prix. That was how she and Angus one day very nearly demolished Mrs. Stone.

Mrs. Stone was a big woman — big in front and big behind — who was not given to nonsense and frippery. She was a stern, hard woman in class, and an even sterner one out of it. The lunch break had just started, and all the students had poured out into the yard and onto the lawns and playing fields. The main corridor was deserted. Jodie had been delayed in her classroom by Mr. Hines, the math teacher, and Angus had been waiting for her impatiently at the door.

"Come on, Jode," he called when she finally emerged. "We're late for the cafeteria. There'll be a line a mile long."

She accelerated past him in the chair. "Come on then," she answered. "You're holding me up."

"*I'm* holding *you* up?" he yelled. "I like that."

She was already three or four yards ahead of him. "Race you down the corridor," she called.

"You're on." He took up the challenge without thinking, even though he knew that school rules forbade running inside the buildings. The long straight stretch ahead looked inviting, and there was not a soul in sight. He accelerated after her.

By the time they were halfway down the straight-away, he was running full tilt and the wheelchair was bowling along like a racing chariot. His breath was hissing between his lips. Jodie glanced side-ways quickly in case he was on the verge of overtaking her, and then leaned forward in her seat as if encouraging the chair to go faster. He was very close.

"Got you," he crowed.

"Like fun."

At that moment, without warning of any sort, Mrs. Stone stepped out of the storeroom and right into their path. She had no idea that Jodie Carpenter, rocketing down the Grand Prix straightaway, was almost upon her. She wasn't even looking. She was having a last word with someone in the storeroom and so she came out more or less backward. Jodie had no time to think or act. The wheelchair was like a hunting hawk at the climax of its swift silent swoop. Mrs. Stone was the quarry — seized, swept off her feet, and carried away in an instant.

It was lucky that Jodie, rather than Angus, had the inside lane nearest the wall, or one of them might have been badly hurt. As it was, Mrs. Stone had time for only one blood-chilling shriek before she was borne off, sitting in Jodie's lap with her legs immodestly up in the air. Jodie cried out too, and Angus swerved sideways spectacularly in his Olympian dash. "Moses," he hissed.

The sudden addition of Mrs. Stone's ample body upset the wheelchair's equilibrium and prevented Jodie from steering or braking properly. For a terrifying moment it seemed certain that they were going to rocket ahead to destruction through the plateglass doors at the end of the corridor.

It was Angus who saved them. With a soccer player's sidelong leap he seized the back of the wheelchair and hung on. It careered breathtakingly from side to side for a second or two—a Grand Prix car completely out of control and in great danger of capsizing and dumping Mrs. Stone violently on the floor—but it slowed down quickly in the process until she was able to find her feet. Then she pressed her big flat-heeled, rubber-soled shoes against the floor, and although she left two wavering black skid marks that the caretaker later found very hard to remove, they acted efficiently as brakes. The wheelchair slowed to a stop and Mrs. Stone was able to get off.

"Well!" she said breathlessly, dusting her skirt as if she had just finished playing in the kindergarten sandpit. "What on earth do you think you're doing?" They knew she was outraged, because the wattles under her chin were wobbling out of control. "You know very well that you are not allowed to run inside the buildings." Then, realizing that the word "run" was hardly appropriate in Jodie's case, she quickly repeated her earlier question. "What on earth were you doing?"

"I . . . I was hurrying to the cafeteria, Mrs. Stone."

"You must never hurry down the corridor, Jodie. That is, you must only hurry *slowly*."

"Yes, Mrs. Stone."

"You could have had a serious accident. We could all have finished up in a . . . in a . . ."

Angus was certain she was about to say "wheelchair" but the sight of Jodie's questioning face threw her into confusion. ". . . in a hospital." Realizing that she wasn't handling things very well, Mrs. Stone decided to retreat. "Off you go to lunch then. And don't let me catch you racing down the corridors again."

"No, Mrs. Stone."

"Do you hear?"

"No, Mrs. Stone. I mean, er, yes, Mrs. Stone."

They both put on suitably contrite expressions and fled. "Gosh, you were lucky," Angus whispered. "You could have knocked the wind right out of her."

Jodie grinned. "Tell you what. She knocked the wind out of me!"

Angus opened the plate-glass door and eyed her as she passed through. "That's a pretty good wheelchair, Jode, really fast and strong."

They both hooted with laughter and escaped outside.

11

THE YEAR PASSED quickly. Jodie's thirteenth birthday came and went, and before long, or so it seemed, her fourteenth was not far off. In spite of the dislocation her illness had caused to the whole family, she was able to get back to some sort of routine at last: up at seven for a hot shower and the slow painful business of getting dressed, into the kitchen with the help of a walking frame for breakfast, off to school with her mother and the wheelchair at half past eight, schoolwork all day, home again with her mother at half past four, a lovely hour or so down at the stables watching Tanya and Monarch from her chair, followed by tea at seven, a bit of homework, and into bed early every night.

Once a month she missed classes to keep an appointment with Dr. Klein, and once a week she had hydrotherapy in the special pool at the hospital. Her father changed his job halfway through the second year of her illness so that he could spend more time at home, but Jodie realized that it was her mother who really carried the burden. She worked at the library for four days a week and spent the fifth day running Jodie to doctors and hospitals and catching up on all the household jobs that hadn't been done. It was such an exhausting routine that she said she almost looked forward to the horse shows they attended every Saturday.

In her heart she knew that the shows were vitally important for Jodie. They gave her an interest, kept her spirits up, jollied her along. Above all, despite the pain, they encouraged her to keep using the joints in her body so that they wouldn't stiffen and freeze up altogether. She stood to pat Monarch's nose or to let him nuzzle her shoulder, and she walked a few steps to eye him off when he was ready for the arena, with Tanya in the saddle. During an event Jodie sometimes stood holding on to the boundary rail at the edge of the oval, following every jump with breathless concentration, cheering with elation or muttering with disappointment. As Dr. Klein would have said, it was a form of therapy, a way of "getting on top of the disease" with her heart and mind, if not with her body. The whole day was often a joy, quite apart from the events in the arena. Jodie's father usually took the portable barbecue and a big parcel of chops, and her mother packed an enormous picnic hamper. Even Alan came along whenever he could to act as chef and coffee maker. The older girls of the district couldn't resist him and hung about the barbecue laughing at his jokes.

Lunch was therefore a lovely interlude in the program. Jodie's mother spread rugs on the grass under the trees and other families came over to join them—the Thompsons, the Abbotts, the Langs, and various horse-riding friends. It became a kind of weekly picnic.

The old rivalry with Amanda Ritchie still went on, of course, but now it was Tanya rather than Jodie who bore the brunt of it. Monarch and Amanda's horse, Superior, were evenly matched, sometimes one winning and sometimes the other. Luckily there were also times when they were both beaten by some other entrant, which Jodie's father said was an excellent thing because it prevented swollen heads.

Although they had so much fun and steady success on the show circuit, it still wasn't easy for Jodie. Her heart ached every time Tanya and Monarch went out onto the oval. She could see herself in Tanya's place, the center of attention and applause, just as she had been on that wonderful day at Greenvale before the terrible disease had crippled her. If Tanya botched a jump, Jodie couldn't help wondering whether she would have made the same mistake. If Monarch pulled a rail, she wondered whether he would have pulled it if she had been riding. And when Tanya won a blue ribbon, Jodie yearned to be out there while the judge draped it around Monarch's neck and handed over the trophy. But she knew that it could never be. All she could do was steel herself and cheer for Tanya.

At the end of the season she had a wonderful surprise. Tanya and her parents came across for a visit one Sunday afternoon, bringing a carton neatly wrapped in blue paper and sealed with tape. They handed it to Jodie.

"For me?" she asked in astonishment. "But it's not Christmas yet, and it isn't my birthday."

"It's something special," Tanya answered.

Jodie had trouble stripping off the tape because of her deformed fingers, but she put up with the pain in order to enjoy the surprise. "I can't imagine what it is," she said, pulling away the wrapping paper at last.

Tanya grinned. "You'll see."

At last Jodie was able to fold back the lid of the carton and peer inside.

She was flabbergasted. It was filled with trophies — half a dozen or more — from the main shows of the year.

"But . . . but they're *yours*," she protested.

Jodie pulled the trophies out one by one and stared in amazement. They were all inscribed with the date and place of the show, and the name of the event. After that, in clear lettering, were the words *Monarch — owned by J. Carpenter.*

Jodie flushed. "But that's not right. You're the person who won them."

"I wouldn't have won anything without Monarch. I would have been stuck home alone, riding a seesaw."

"They're yours all the same."

"I've got the other half — and all the ribbons."

"The other half? What the heck are you talking about?"

"I've got as many as you have. We've each got half of everything that Monarch won."

Jodie shook her head incredulously. "Really?"

"Yes. Except mine are inscribed *Monarch — ridden by Tanya Thompson.*"

Jodie looked round with a suspicious grin. "I wonder how that came about?"

Her father coughed and Mr. Thompson hastily gazed out of the window.

Jodie's mother laughed. "Oh come on, you two. There's no need to look like a couple of shy little schoolboys." She turned to Jodie. "Of course they cooked it up. But it was a nice idea."

Jodie hugged them all in turn. She was afraid to say anything in case she started blubbering and made an ass of herself.

12

JODIE'S FOURTEENTH birthday ushered in a time of celebration. It was followed soon afterward by Alan's twenty-first, and then by Christmas and the New Year's vacation.

Her father had rented a cottage by the beach for three weeks from the beginning of January, and they all prepared to have the laziest time of their lives. Her father and mother said they needed to recharge their batteries, Alan needed a break before starting his final year at the university, and the doctors said Jodie would benefit from a vacation by the sea. She was growing up, and perhaps in two or three years' time she could begin to have surgery on some of her deformed limbs.

"We won't even bother to take your wheelchair," her father said as they were preparing to leave. "You couldn't use it on the beach anyway. Not in the soft sand."

She agreed. "No, I guess not."

"You can putter about inside, using your walking frame if you have to, or sunbathe out on the patio. And if you want to go down to the beach Alan and I will carry you. We'll even dunk you in the sea if you like."

"Don't you dare."

"It would do you good," Alan said. "They say seawater can cure anything — even dandruff."

The vacation turned out to be even better than they had expected. They took every day as it came: sleeping late, getting up when they liked, lounging about, going for drives inland, reading, or lying on the sand. Jodie and her mother were treated like guests. If they wanted to sleep late, they were left undisturbed. If meals were needed, the men prepared them. If they wanted to lounge on the beach, Alan carried Jodie. Her father even offered to carry her mother, but she told him not to be stupid. "If you try that sort of nonsense you'll ruin your back," she said, "and then you'll be a pain in the neck for the rest of the week."

Sometimes they ate hamburgers and drank Coke

in the shade of the old jetty. "No wonder you've got arthritis," Alan said, mimicking Granny Hooper as he munched hungrily. "All this junk food. Fills your bones with acid."

"Don't scoff," his mother said.

Alan went on regardless. "By the way," he said innocently, "I met a camel breeder from Kapunda who has over fifty cam—"

His mother threw an orange at him. "Oh, shut up, Alan."

Despite the success of the vacation it was inevitable that there would be times of hurt and unhappiness for Jodie. She was always in pain—during every minute of every hour of every day—and there was no way by which other people could know how severe it was. She could say, "It's very bad today," and there was nothing they could answer except, "We're sorry." Or she could say, "It's not quite as bad as it was yesterday," and they would answer, "That's good," utterly unaware of her meaning—that the pain was still fiendish but not as doubly fiendish as it had been the day before, or as it might be again tomorrow.

There was also the embarrassment of explanation. One day she was in the shallow water near the shore where Alan, in his best Granny Hooper voice, had finally persuaded her to sit. The water

101

was pleasantly warm, and the tiny ripples rolling over her knees were as soothing as the gentlest of spa pools. She was sitting up with her hands spread on either side of her because she couldn't bear the pain if she pressed them into the sand behind her and leaned back as she would have liked to do. She was glad that the incoming ripples hid the lower part of her body and disguised the knock-kneed angle of her legs.

Alan had left her sitting there by herself for a few minutes while he trudged up to the kiosk. She was wearing a black swimsuit and dark sunglasses, and despite the effect of sand, salt, and sun, her black hair had not altogether lost its gloss. She looked pretty. Obviously other people on the beach thought so too, because a boy of fifteen or sixteen suddenly detached himself from a group of teenagers who were playing volleyball nearby and came panting up to her, spraying sand as he ran. "Hi. Want a game?"

She was startled and looked up hastily. "No. No, thanks."

"Come on." He was good-looking and he seemed nice.

She smiled fleetingly. "Thanks, but no."

He persisted. "Don't be shy. The fellows in our mob are okay."

She was embarrassed and her face flushed. "Oh, it's not that."

"What then? You don't want to be sitting here all alone all day. Not someone like you."

She was getting desperate. If he had been vulgar and demanding, she would have told him to get lost. But he was kind and genuine, if just a bit pushy and boyishly overenergetic. Clearly he had no idea of her handicap. How could he?

"Come on," he said again, holding out his hand as if to help her to her feet. "You'll have a ball."

She looked up directly at him. "Look," she said, "I'd love to, but . . ." She paused, lost in mid sentence. What could she say? What words could she possibly use? If she told him she had arthritis, it would be meaningless, even if he believed her. If she said she'd been crippled by a disease, he would probably shrink away from her as though she had leprosy. Her mind was groping for the right expression.

"I'd love to, but . . . but I can't run and jump like ordinary girls." It came out in a rush — something she had never said to any boy before.

He paused, eyeing her intently. "Really? On the level?"

"Yes."

"You have an accident or something?"

103

"Something like that."

He stood uncertainly for a moment, his doubt written clearly on his face. "That's awful," he said. And then, as if he'd had a sudden inspiration, "Can you swim?"

"Not really."

"Then why are you . . . ?"

Luckily he didn't have time to finish the question, because Alan came striding back just then with two melting ice creams that were sending rivulets of chocolate down his fingers. "Hi," he said to the stranger.

"Oh, hi."

Jodie almost choked with relief.

"Sorry about the mess," Alan said.

"That's okay."

"Ice cream is bad for you anyway. It'll fill your bones with acid." His eyes twinkled.

"I'd better go," the stranger said. "See you."

"See you," Jodie answered. "And thanks." As she watched him lope across the loose sand to join his friends again, she envied his energy and the beautiful movement of his body.

"Who's that?" Alan asked.

"No idea."

They finished their ice creams in silence and washed their hands in the sea.

"What now?" he asked.

"Take me home, would you please, Al?"

"Sure."

He picked her up lightly and tramped up the beach toward the cottage. Looking over his shoulder, Jodie could see the strange boy standing stock-still, staring after them in amazement. The expression on his face made her want to cry.

13

AS SOON AS they arrived home from the beach at the end of their vacation, the routine of the year swallowed them up again. Jodie's mother and father had to start work, Alan returned to the university, and within a week Jodie found herself back at Hillbank High.

Early in February Tanya began working Monarch again to prepare him for the next season's shows. He was edgy after his long break, and she had trouble settling him down. He was also too fat. On hot afternoons his coat glistened with sweat after just a few minutes, and the flies were so bad that he was forever stamping his feet and tossing his head even when he was supposed to be well-behaved on the lunging rein. Because there wasn't much shade in his little paddock, Jodie suggested that Tanya should leave the stable door open every morning so that he could come and go as he pleased during the heat of the day.

The heat didn't help Jodie, despite the old saying that summer was a better time for people with arthritis. The inflammation in her arms and hips flared up badly, and even the hydrotherapy sessions in the pool failed to do anything for her.

One morning things were so bad that her mother suggested she should stay home from school for the day. The weather forecasters were predicting high temperatures with nasty northerly winds that were likely to make things very uncomfortable for Jodie at school in her wheelchair. The fact that she would be home by herself didn't worry her. Her mother had to dash off to town and her father was in Melbourne on business for a few days.

As usual her mother was in a desperate hurry. She left the dishes in the sink and rushed about looking for her bag and car keys. She kissed Jodie hastily. "Look after yourself, love. If you need anything at all, just telephone me at the library."

"Yes, Mum."

"There's some salad and orange juice in the fridge."

"Thanks, Mum."

"You can get it for yourself, can't you?"

"Sure—give me time."

"I may be home a bit late. I'm having the car serviced. They have to put in a new gabbet or basket or something."

Jodie laughed. "A gasket?"

"I guess that's it." Her mother glanced at the clock. "Gosh, I must fly. Be careful, love. Don't forget to take your pills."

"No, Mum." Jodie stood leaning against the kitchen sink. "'Bye," she called. There was silence for a moment and then she heard the engine of her mother's car rev suddenly. A minute later the sound dwindled down the drive.

Jodie hesitated, wondering what to do next. In the end she decided to attempt to wash the dishes. She knew she had to be careful because plates and cups tended to fall out of her hands without warning, and her mother was always grumbling about breakages. She slowly pushed one of the kitchen stools into place at the sink and sat down. Then she dribbled in some detergent, took the tap opener from the windowsill, and filled the sink.

For a while she just sat with her hands in the sudsy water, enjoying the soothing warmth. She looked at her hands—big swollen nodules on her knuckles, thumbs thick and painful, little fingers misshapen and sticking out stiffly at an angle, other fingers arched and ending in a sudden kink at the last joint—the "swan's neck," as her doctors called it. Then she took the breakfast dishes item by item, washed them slowly, and put them on the rack to dry.

The marker on the kitchen calendar above the windowsill pointed to the sixteenth of February. It was the day people all over Australia were soon to call Ash Wednesday.

For a while Jodie was completely at loose ends. She didn't want to go back to bed, because it was already too hot, and doing schoolwork on a day like this was unthinkable. There was no point in eating, because she wasn't hungry; there was nothing worthwhile on the radio, and if she tried to sit out in the sunshine to warm her painful bones, she knew she would be baked by the heat and sandblasted by the gritty wind. And her greatest pastime—talking on the telephone—was quite out of the question because Tanya and Lynn and every other friend she could think of were all at school.

Although her wheelchair was standing near the front door, she didn't really need it inside the house. She could move about quite safely, if slowly

109

and painfully, by using her walking frame or by holding on to the furniture. In the end she took a book called *Space Devils*, which she had started reading the previous day, and sat down in her armchair to try to relax. The chair was specially made, with strong armrests so that she could lever herself up from a sitting to a standing position, and it had a kind of tray that swung across in front of her in a horizontal or inclined position. It was useful for all kinds of things: holding cups of tea, mugs of soup, or plates of food, acting as a desk for homework or games, or an angled reading bench to hold books or papers. It spared her some of the pain that came from holding up a book or magazine with her hands.

The story was exciting. By eleven o'clock she was so engrossed in the evil of the demons and their computer-controlled existence that she jerked with fright when the telephone rang shrilly at her elbow. It was her mother calling to check that everything was all right, and to say that she had taken the car to the garage directly across the road from the library. It wouldn't be ready until four o'clock, so she probably would not be home until five.

"That's okay," Jodie said.

Her mother changed the subject. "What's it like up there—the weather?"

"The weather?" Jodie hadn't really given any thought to it. She hastily looked out the window to where the trees were being lashed about by the wind. Little scurries of dust were flying up from the dirt track that led across to the Thompsons' place.

"Pretty windy," she said.

"And hot?" her mother asked.

"I guess so." Again Jodie had no real awareness of it because she had been sheltered inside the house.

"It's awful down here. They say the wind's blowing at more than forty miles an hour and the temperature is a hundred and four degrees—and set to go higher."

"Gosh."

"So stay inside, love. Switch on the air conditioner if you like."

"Okay, Mum."

"I'll get home as soon as I can, depending on the car."

"No worries. I'm all right."

"I'd better go now. Good-bye dear."

" 'Bye, Mum."

The sudden interruption had broken Jodie's concentration. She put down her book, pushed away the swivel tray so that it folded down at the side

111

of the chair, and stood up. For a minute or two the pain in her legs bit fiercely. It was always like that when she got up after a long period of inactivity. Her joints seemed to have stiffened in the meantime and objected to being straightened out.

She hobbled across to her walking frame and used it to move more confidently into the living room, where she stood at the big picture window, looking out at the sweeping countryside beyond. It was a lovely view — rolling hills and valleys, with dark masses of trees bunched along the slopes and the crests of the ridges as far as she could see. Even in February, when the whole state had been baked in summer heat for so long that everything was brittle and the grass under the trees was as gray as death, there was still much that was very beautiful about the Adelaide Hills.

She could feel the force of the wind now, harrying the corners of the house. The wooden garden gate was swinging wildly and crashing against the latch. As usual, her mother had left it open in her morning rush, and now the gale was slowly pounding it to pieces. Jodie could sense the heat more strongly too, bearing against the walls and roof of the house and slowly seeping inside. The sight of the writhing trees and spinning dust and the spread of a strange haze across the sky made her uneasy. There was something menacing about it, something wild and elemental. For no real reason she suddenly shuddered and turned away.

The heat was making her thirsty. She shuffled through to the kitchen with her walking frame, went to the fridge, and very carefully took out the carton of orange juice. Carrying it over to the sink, opening the flanges of the spout, and pouring out a glassful were all difficult tasks, but she managed them without disaster. Then she folded back the spout and replaced the carton. She took a long time over the drink, using her left hand to lift the glass to her mouth, because her right elbow was so stiff that she tended to dribble and spill drinks if she tried to use it.

She couldn't help seeing the kitchen clock in front of her as she was drinking. The time was half past eleven. Although she didn't know it, the first alarm had just gone through to the headquarters of the Country Fire Service. Fire had broken out at McLaren Flat and was sweeping toward Kuitpo Forest.

The Ash Wednesday holocaust had started.

14

JODIE DRAGGED herself back into the living room and sat down by the window. From her chair she could see most of their little farm: the garden in front of the house, the small horse paddocks beyond it, the stables, the dam a few hundred yards down the gully. A thick belt of scrub spread in a semicircle through other properties across the slopes above. It blanketed most of the high ground, dotted here and there with houses among the trees, and then swung around in an arc past the Thompsons' place to Greenvale itself.

She realized how lucky she was to be living in a place like this. If it hadn't been for the disease that had somehow selected her—if she were still healthy and able to ride Monarch — she would have been the happiest girl in Australia.

The wind was raging now, rampaging the landscape. The ornamental shrubs in the garden were being savaged, their leaves torn and stripped, and the big trees behind the stables and all along the northern and western boundaries at the back of the house were threshing wildly. In the distance they looked like the figures of mourners in a play, flinging their arms about in grief. The heat against the glass was intense. Jodie pulled the curtains partly across the windows, almost losing her balance in the process. It was a timely warning. She knew that if she fell it would be very hard — perhaps impossible — for her to get up on her feet again.

Although she wasn't particularly hungry, she needed to eat something before she swallowed her midday quota of pills, so she hobbled back to the kitchen and decided on a slice of bread and butter with some of the salad her mother had left for her. Spreading the butter was always a hard task because of her swollen knuckles and aching wrists. They prevented her from turning the knife or applying pressure. Fortunately it didn't matter much when she was by herself. It was only when other people were watching that she felt embarrassed about her clumsiness.

As she was preparing her lunch, she was quite unaware that fires had also broken out at Clare and at Tea Tree Gully a few minutes earlier. And when she was clearing up after lunch, she could not know that a huge outbreak near Lucindale had begun engulfing the forests of the South East. It was not until another hour had gone by that her first real fears began. By then Mount Osmond and Greenhill near Adelaide had exploded into flames, and yet another outbreak was threatening the countryside near Hahndorf.

The sight of smoke, a vast red-brown cloud across the sky, and an eerie light that somehow suggested the end of the world, suddenly made her think of herself. She had never been in a bushfire before, but she had heard and read enough about them to be afraid. Without hesitation she shuffled over to the phone to call her mother. It wasn't until she had dialed several digits with her clumsy fingers that she realized something was wrong. She lowered the receiver and gazed at it in dismay. There was no dial tone. She shook it, thumped the cradle, and listened again. No sound. The phone was dead.

A sense of dread swept her, a terrible feeling of isolation. She took her walking frame and went out onto the verandah as quickly as she could. It was like opening a furnace door. The heat and

116

the wind assaulted her with such a searing blast that she automatically lifted her left hand as if to shield her face. Coming and going on the gusts she could hear the Greenvale fire siren wailing in the far distance. It rose and fell, rose and fell, going on and on ceaselessly. It was a cry for help, a call for more and more firefighters — volunteers, townspeople, anybody. There was no need for Jodie to imagine what was going on. She knew the answer.

As she stood there uncertainly gazing at the copper-colored sky, she was aware of movement in the lower paddock. It was Monarch, retreating from the water trough and seeking shelter in his stable. He walked with his head down against the fury of the wind. At the sight of him Jodie started suddenly in fear. If the fires came near the stables, he would be in mortal danger.

She was torn by terrible doubts, wondering whether she should go down in her wheelchair and try to lock Monarch in his stable. But that would be stupid, because if the fire did come he would be trapped, with no hope of escape. She had heard of horses caught in stable fires like that. Yet if he was running free, he might panic and hurt himself by blundering into logs, trenches, or barbed-wire fences.

She went back inside and switched on the kitchen

radio to try to get some news. The station was playing music, which was reassuring because it suggested that life in South Australia was normal.

In actual fact, if Jodie had only known, life in the Adelaide Hills was not normal; it was in a state of catastrophe. Gigantic walls of flame, sometimes spawning incandescent fireballs like explosive outbursts from the rim of the sun, were roaring out of control in half a dozen places. There was tumult everywhere: trees exploding into great pyres, pipes melting, animals stampeding, fire trucks racing in a vast turmoil of smoke and heat and fear and desperate bravery. Houses and cars were burning, people were dying, sheep and cattle and horses were being engulfed before they could flee.

For the fires were traveling so fast that there was no time for the defenders to plan and regroup. The wind and the heat were turning gullies into blast furnaces, buildings into incinerators. Police were already blocking off the highways and closing roads, if only to prevent people from driving into the inferno.

As the fires threatened towns and hamlets in the hills, urgent orders went out to those in peril. People fleeing the fury gathered in halls or on sports fields, often with nothing but the grimy clothes they were wearing, sometimes clutching a cat or a dog or a few pitiful possessions, while the fire-fighters stood with their backs to the town, ready to do battle with the fearful dragon that was roaring down on them.

That was how it was at Greenvale. Sergeant Giles and Constable Shepherd raced about the country-side, using their radio to try to keep in touch with the latest news, and telling people they had less than five minutes to flee their homes. As they hurtled from place to place, they tried to keep track of as many local families as they could, especially those out on the farms or in the scrubs. Sergeant Giles was driving furiously with one hand, holding the microphone in the other, giving radio messages at the same time as he was checking names with Constable Shepherd.

"The Holts?" he said. "The Wilsons, Blacks, and Solomons?"

"Okay," Constable Shepherd answered. "They've all been told to go into Greenvale."

"Spatafora and Angelakus?"

"They've both been warned."

"Harris and Menzel?"

"Nobody home there."

119

"Thompsons?"

"Tanya's at school and Bob and Gloria are in town."

"Carpenters?"

"It'll be the same with them. Ben's in Melbourne on business and Helen's at work."

"And young Jodie — the crippled girl?"

"She'll be at school too."

Sergeant Giles looked out of the window as they raced along. "Maybe we ought to take a quick run out there, just to be sure."

"Have we got time? We have to check the hospital, remember?"

Just then a message, broken up by all kinds of noise, came urgently over the radio. "The fire's on Wilson's Bridge, traveling straight for Greenvale."

Constable Shepherd glanced back hastily. "We'd better get out of here," he yelled, "or we'll be trapped."

There was no need to stress the point. Sergeant Giles had already swung the police car around, pressed the accelerator down hard, and hurtled back toward Greenvale. Neither of them knew that Jodie Carpenter was at home alone, cut off from help.

The next ugly warning sign came from Jodie's radio — not from a dramatic message by the announcer but from sudden silence. At one moment music was playing normally, and at the next there was nothing at all, not even a hum or spatter of static. A second later Jodie realized that the fridge and the air conditioner had stopped too — all at the same instant. There was no electricity. The power lines were down.

Filled with sudden panic, she dragged herself hastily back to her own room, seized her pocket radio, and switched it on. It ran on batteries. By coincidence the announcer had just started giving an urgent news flash. All the fires throughout the state were out of control. There was immense destruction in the timber areas of the South East. A message that Hills residents should return to their own homes was now being contradicted. The fires had traveled too fast. Roads were closed and police were not letting anyone through. There were reports of deaths and injuries, but in the confusion it was difficult to get accurate details. The area around Greenvale was being evacuated.

Greenvale! For Jodie the news was like an electric shock. If the fire was threatening the town, it would soon be roaring toward her. And then, in her turmoil of uncertainty and dread, a new fear seized her. Monarch had no means of escape. If the fire swept down on them, he would be burned to death.

It was a possibility so appalling that it swept everything else from Jodie's mind — even her own safety.

Only one thought remained. Somehow Monarch had to be saved.

15

THE CENTRAL thought in Jodie's mind was the dam. It was still half full of water, and the banks around it were bare of trees, although dry grass almost surrounded it. If she could get Monarch down there somehow, he might be safe.

She struggled over to her wheelchair, threw herself into it, and drove hastily to the laundry door at the back of the house, where long ago her father had built a concrete ramp for her. The door tended to jam and she had to heave herself up into a standing position to wrench it free. The pain in her hands was excruciating.

As soon as she was outside, she trundled down the ramp, the hot wind striking her like a slap in the face. At the bottom of the ramp she turned sharply and headed for the stables. As she did so, she gasped. The whole of the ridge above Greenvale was a line of fire as far as she could see—a tidal wave of flame. Smoke was billowing up from it in swirling surges. Everywhere trees were bursting into fireballs, and huge sheets of flame were breaking away and rising into the air like monsters with fiery wings.

"Oh my God," Jodie said under her breath, and sent the wheelchair careering down the track toward the stables.

Luckily, Monarch was still in his stall. If he had been out in the paddock, fidgeting and moving about, it would have been far more difficult. There was a concrete apron in front of the stables, which made it easy for her to maneuver the chair from place to place. She brought it up to the stable door and called reassuringly. "Steady. Steady, boy." He was uneasy, sensing fear in her voice and danger in the air.

Jodie knew there was no hope of saddling him. She couldn't raise her arms to the level of her own shoulders, let alone lift a saddle onto a horse's back and then tighten the girth straps with a strong pull. She couldn't get a bridle over his ears either, especially when he tossed his head impatiently, as he

124

always did. She would have to hold on to his halter and try to ride him bareback. The dam was only two or three hundred yards down the gully, and he knew the way well enough. But first she would have to get up on his back.

That was how her torture began. She eased herself up out of the wheelchair, edged her way inside the stall, and pulled the half door partly shut behind her. "Steady, boy," she said again. She was angry with herself for forgetting to bring a lump of sugar. She took him by the halter, hanging on perilously for support, and coaxed him forward until he was standing near his feedbin. Her plan was to use a bucket as a step to the bin, and the bin as a step up to Monarch's back. She knew it was dangerous but she had no choice. The air was thick and acrid, heavy with dust and heat and rolling smoke.

"Here, boy," she said soothingly. "Steady now."

She had to use all her strength to haul herself onto the bin. The pain was so bad that she winced. But she managed the climb somehow and stood there for a few seconds, supporting herself by means of the waterpipe that ran along the wall to the trough nearby.

"Steady," she murmured yet again, bracing herself for the final test. She had to swing her right leg over the horse's back and then wriggle into a

125

riding position. After that it would just be a matter of guiding him out through the stable door and down the track to the dam. She hadn't even given any thought to anything beyond that—how she was going to get off or how she hoped to hold him. At present all that mattered was his safety.

The pain of suddenly putting all her weight on her left leg and at the same time forcibly swinging her right leg upward was so indescribable that she cried out. She couldn't manage it. It was simply impossible to lift her leg up and over. Her knee and hip had so little movement left that, before her foot was even halfway up, they seemed to lock in place, as rigid as wood. Three times she tried to force the leg over Monarch's back, even pushing and lifting feebly with her right hand, but it was hopeless. For a second or two she seemed to hang there with tears of pain and frustration welling in her eyes, and then Monarch moved away. Like a novice sailor caught with one foot on the jetty and one in a moving boat, her body momentarily felt as if it was being split in two, and then she fell heavily to the ground.

Fortunately, Monarch didn't plunge about, or he would have trampled her as she lay there. For a while she was stunned. Her whole body seemed to have been shattered. Her shoulders, wrists, hands, hips, and knees were high points of agony in a sea of pain. She wondered vaguely whether her arms or legs were broken, joints dislocated, senses concussed, but the terrible reality of her situation remained clearly in her mind. She groaned and sat up.

The struggle to get back on her feet used up the last of her strength. With one elbow on the bucket and the misshapen fingers of her left hand on the edge of the feedbin, she pressed her back against the wall and, with a stupendous effort, started to jack herself up. Her breath rushed through her clenched teeth. It was the supreme trial of her will. Slowly she rose up until her quaking knees were holding her upright again. She stood there for a second or two, clinging unsteadily to the stable door. Outside, the air was thicker than ever with ash and scudding smoke. Jodie realized now that there was no hope of riding Monarch. She would have to lead him down to the dam — from the wheelchair.

Seizing a rope from the rack by the door, she hastily started tying one end to the ring on Monarch's halter, her clumsy fingers taking even longer than usual. Then she pushed open the door, climbed aboard her wheelchair, and led him out. He was fractious and afraid, prancing and snorting at the sight of the flying ash and the smell of the smoke.

There was worse to come, for as they rounded the end of the stables, they suddenly came into full view of the holocaust above Greenvale. It looked like the death throes of the universe—an awful color like blood blanketing the sky, an inferno of flame beneath. The whole world seemed to be writhing and dying. Vaguely Jodie realized that the fire was sweeping down on the homes of her neighbors—the Langs and Abbotts and Thompsons—but her mind was so numbed by anguish and exhaustion that she couldn't really comprehend the horror of it all.

She clung desperately to Monarch's rope and set the wheelchair going as fast as she could down the gully toward the dam. Unlike the smooth track that ran from the house to the stables, the way was rough and uneven, furrowed with little washaways. She had to be careful not to rush headlong into one of them and tip or stall. For the first hundred yards of their journey the track ran under a canopy of trees, but then it broke out into open grassland with a scatter of bushes and thistles.

Jodie began to feel a glimmer of hope. She kept talking to Monarch, trying to soothe him whenever he was startled by something and tried to pull back.

The fire was barely half a mile away now. Under the red dome of the sky the clouds of smoke were billowing above them. They rolled over Jodie's head, swirling, expanding, sucked outward and upward like the blast from an atomic bomb. The nearness of the terror was overwhelming. Monarch started to snort and rear.

"Steady, steady," Jodie called. "Good boy. It's not far now."

They were within a hundred yards of the dam, eighty yards, seventy yards. If nothing further had happened as Jodie fled jolting and veering down the track with Monarch, she might have succeeded in leading him to safety, although even then she might not have been able to hold him during the last terrible moments. But when they were within fifty yards of the dam, disaster struck. Five panic-stricken horses suddenly galloped out of the smoke and went stampeding down the gully below the dam toward the Greenbank road. They were fleeing blindly. Behind them the inferno had swept over the farms where Amanda and Jessica lived, engulfing Tanya's house and wolfing up the belt of scrub below.

The sudden onrush of hoofs was too much for Monarch. He reared, whinnying, and then plunged away wildly. Jodie cried out, holding frantically on to the rope, but she was powerless. Monarch's violent leap pulled her sideways. An instant later the wheelchair capsized, the rope was torn from her hands, and Monarch went thundering after the mob.

"*Monarch!*" Jodie screamed. "*Monarch, come back!*"

It was a cry lost in a world that was dying. She lay where she had fallen, her elbows bleeding, her body wracked with agony. And from the west the inferno bore down on her.

16

A T ABOUT HALF past three, when the true horror of the fires began to be known all over Australia, Jodie's father telephoned urgently from Melbourne. The girl who answered the phone at the library said that Jodie's mother was out — over at the garage, hastily trying to get her car back. "The fires are bad," the girl said. "There are news flashes over the radio all the time."

"How bad?"

"Terrible. Half of South Australia seems to be alight."

"They're certainly bad over here," Jodie's father said. "Half of Victoria is alight too."

"Can I take a message?" the girl asked.

"Just say I'm coming home straight away. I'll take the first plane I can get."

At the garage, Jodie's mother was in a frenzy. The mechanics who were working on her car said it wouldn't be ready for at least another hour.

"But I need it now," she shouted. "I don't care whether it's fixed or not, just so long as I can drive it."

"Sorry," they said, "we've got the head off."

"Well, put it back on."

"That'll take quite a while."

She put her hands up to her hair as if about to tear out a fistful of it. "Can you lend me a car, then? Jodie's home alone, and they say there are fires all around Greenvale. I just have to get up there. I have to leave *now*."

The men were sympathetic. "We can lend you a utility truck, if that's any good to you."

"That'll do."

"It's a manual, not an automatic."

"Doesn't matter. I can drive it."

"Better be careful."

Jodie's mother roared off up the street toward Glen Osmond — but she didn't get far. There were roadblocks on all the roads into the Hills.

"Sorry," the police sergeant said. "We can't let you through."

"But I live up there," she shouted.

"Sorry, not even residents."

"Look, my daughter's home alone."

"She will have been evacuated by now."

"How do you know? The phone lines are all dead."

"Sorry, madam, we can't allow anyone through."

She was furious with frustration. "Sergeant, I *must* get through."

"In good time, madam. We'll open the roads as soon as it's safe to proceed."

Jodie's mother drove back to the library. She was tense with fear and aching inwardly with a terrible feeling of guilt. What on earth had made her suggest that Jodie should stay at home by herself? Who would have left a handicapped daughter without help on such a day? She tried to telephone Jodie's father in Melbourne, but he had already left for the airport. All she could do was bite her fingernails and listen white faced as horror after horror unfolded on the radio from eyewitnesses and reporters in helicopters and fire engines. And so the terrible afternoon dragged on toward evening. Although she finally got her car back, it was of little use because the roads were still closed.

When Jodie's father landed at Adelaide Airport, he hired a taxi and rushed out to the library. By a stroke of luck he caught his wife just as she was about to set off on another attempt to get through. "Any news?" he called as he sprang from the cab.

She gave him a stricken look. "Jodie's home alone, and the fires have swept through the hills near Greenvale."

He blanched. "Oh my God," was all he could say.

Jodie's mother broke down. "The phone is out," she sobbed. "I've been trying and trying to contact her. The roads are all closed. They won't let anyone through."

He seized her by the arm. "Come on," he said. "We're going home, roadblocks or no roadblocks."

This time permission was granted and they raced off up the highway. As they entered the Hills, they gazed dumbfounded at the devastated landscape. It was a hell of desolation: blackened trees to the horizon, the smoking ruins of houses, stumps burning like the remnants of funeral pyres. Here and there fire still flared on the branches of high trees — grotesque arms semaphoring their messages in flame. And sometimes they could glimpse a red glow through the blackened brick openings of burned-out windows as if a hearth fire had just been lit for winter visitors coming in to spend the night, but the rooms were roofless and the furniture was ash.

"Oh God. Oh God," Jodie's father kept saying.

As they neared Greenvale there were more and more vehicles on the road — fire engines, water tankers, utility trucks, police cars, and even one or two big transports carrying bulldozers, graders, and other heavy equipment. They were directed to the town center by a policeman at a roadblock outside the town. "They've set up a local relief depot in the hall," he said. "You'll be able to get the latest news there."

"But our daughter—"

"I'm sure they'll be able to help you. They saved the town, you know. A miracle, really."

Jodie's father drove on into Greenvale like a man demented. The scene at the hall was like a clearing station at a battlefield. Dr. Manners and Dr. Harper were treating the injured: bandaging arms and legs, examining burns, putting drops into eyes that were red and weeping from smoke, ash, and cinders.

Jodie's father and mother pushed forward. They could hear scraps of conversation, phrases, words — all telling their own horrifying stories. "All gone — house, sheds, everything. . ."; "like a blowtorch . . ."; "caught in their truck and burned to death where they were . . ."; "five thousand sheep and all the cattle and horses . . ."; "no news yet but they fear the worst . . ."

At that moment Jodie's father caught sight of Oscar Hoffmann, their one-time riding instructor, who was the leader of the local fire team. He had just come in exhausted from what he called "the battlefront." He was covered with cinders and soot. "We've checked it," he croaked. "I think we can hold it now."

Jodie's father rushed over to him. "Oscar, what about our place?"

Oscar shook his head and looked at him sadly with his singed eyebrows and bloodshot eyes. "Sorry, Ben. There was nothing we could do — your place, Thompsons', Langs', Ritchies', Abbotts' . . . The fire was traveling at forty miles an hour. We didn't even get out there."

"Gone?"

"All gone."

Jodie's father groaned. "Jodie . . ."

Oscar Hoffman misunderstood. "The children are safe. At Hillbank they kept all the kids back at the school. Best thing they ever did."

"Don't you understand?" Jodie's mother wailed. "Jodie was home all day. She didn't go to school."

Oscar stared at them. "Oh God," he said. Although he was sagging with weariness, he turned and went straight back to the fire truck. "I'll go out and check."

"I'm coming too," Jodie's father said.

"So am I." Jodie's mother was already ahead of them.

Oscar caught up with her and seized her by the arm. "I think maybe, Helen, it would be better if you didn't."

"I'm coming," she said stubbornly. "And if you try to stop me, I'll follow in my own car."

"You can't take a car on that road. Not yet. Better come with us, then."

They climbed into the cabin of the truck and drove off up the street. The police waved them through, warning them about hot spots where trees were still burning at the side of the road. Beyond the town they passed the same kind of hellish desolation as before: blackened scrub, smoldering houses, charred carcasses of cattle, burning fence posts. The sun had set and an eerie twilight lay over the devastation. The wind had swung around to the southwest.

Oscar and Jodie's father and mother sat side by side. Nobody spoke. And so at last they ground their way up the slope and turned into the driveway that led to the house. Although the light was draining from the sky, they could see only too well what lay ahead. Smoke was still wreathing up from the blackened trees behind the spot where the stables had been. All that remained of them was a pile of rubble and a few twisted sheets of roofing iron.

Finally they reached the house. Only two walls and the brick chimney were standing—the stark skeleton of the building that had once been home. Nothing else had survived. Jodie's father and mother sat staring through the windshield, numb with shock and horror.

"Oh no," Jodie's mother kept saying, shaking her head and speaking in a strange whisper. "No, oh no."

Oscar switched off the engine and seized a big flashlight from under the seat. "Wait here," he said.

They watched him as he walked up the fire-blackened path to the aperture that had been the front door. He stood there for a while, flashing the beam of light over the ruins, and then walked forward slowly, scuffing up puffs of ash with his big boots. He was searching for something that he couldn't find.

When he finally turned to go back to the truck, he saw that Jodie's mother and father had followed him. They were standing on what had been the verandah.

"Nothing," he said simply.

Jodie's father seemed to take a deep breath. "Nothing at all?"

"No."

There was silence again, stunned and unbelieving. "D'you . . . d'you mean we're not even going to find her body?" Jodie's mother whispered.

"It was hotter than a furnace," Oscar said at last. "Some people say it reached thirty-six hundred degrees Fahrenheit. Steel melted like butter. The heat turned everything into ash. . . ."

Jodie's mother gave a choking sob and turned away with her hands over her face.

"I'm sorry," Oscar said, his big shoulders drooping with weariness and sorrow. "There was nothing anyone could do."

It was true. There was nothing anyone could do. It had all been done.

17

THAT NIGHT Jodie's name was added to the list of those who had lost their lives in the fire. Friends and neighbors came up to console her father and mother, wringing their hands in silent grief, murmuring sympathy, sharing the tragedy together. Tanya, especially, could not come to terms with it. She sat by herself, hunched up in a corner of the hall, sobbing silently hour after hour.

Throughout the evening more and more tragedies came to light — stories of others who had perished, some in their own houses, some while fleeing in cars, some while fighting the inferno. Nobody yet knew exactly how many. The homeless were put up for the night in all kinds of emergency places: the town hall, the primary school, the convent, even the council chambers and the mayor's parlor. Most of them lay on the bare floors in the clothes they were wearing, often stinking of smoke and the stench of charred cloth. They were the refugees of the holocaust.

In the darkness before dawn, when Jodie's mother had at last fallen asleep after Dr. Manners had given her some sleeping tablets, Jodie's father rose from the floor and tiptoed quietly outside. Heartbroken, he walked quickly down the street to the car and drove off up the road. He wanted to go back by himself to the place Jodie had loved, the place he had bought for *her*, the place where she had known so much happiness with Monarch before disease had crippled her. What had happened to Monarch? he wondered. In the turmoil and tragedy of the previous night nobody had even asked the question.

As he turned up the track between the fire-blackened trees, the wash of dawn across the sky began to lighten, slowly unfolding the desolation around him. He drove up to the ruins of the house, as he and Oscar had done the night before, and walked around it slowly. What was he really looking for? he asked himself. The funeral pyre of his own daughter? He peered at the ruins, looking for detail that wasn't there, amazed at the way everything had simply disappeared.

That, he thought, looking directly at an empty space, was where the heavy cedar dining table used to stand. They had scrimped and saved for five years before they could afford to buy it. And now what a ridiculously tiny heap of ash it made — hardly enough to fill a dustpan. There was not a trace of a book, not a splinter of furniture, not a scrap of cloth or leather, not even a molten bit of plastic. Nothing but ashes, ashes, ashes.

He turned and walked down the track toward the ruined stables. Behind him the imminent sunrise trembled along the crests of the hills where the remnants of the burned trees stood up starkly like twisted black sticks. As he approached the ruins, he trod fearfully, expecting at any moment to see a mound of burned flesh — the carcass of Monarch. But there was nothing.

He circled around, stepping carefully over the fence wires that lay sprawled on the ground where the posts had been burned out. A strange silence lay over the place, unbroken by the usual busy sounds of the morning — birds and insects and animals. It seemed a dead land. Only once was there a faint call like the distant cry of a waterbird. Perhaps an ibis or a heron had escaped somehow in a creek or waterhole.

What was to happen now, he asked himself — without Jodie, without a home, without even a fence or a post or a tree? What was the point of anything?

He moved out into the open beyond the ruined stables. Some of the logs were still burning, their undersides glowing with red coals. Thin wreaths of smoke curled up mockingly in the morning air. His eyes watered — and not from the smoke alone. He moved a short distance down the track that led to the dam, peering away to the right across the face of the slope to try to see what remained of the Thompsons' place, or the Langs'.

There was nothing. He turned and was about to walk back the way he had come when his eye caught sight of something farther down the track. It was debris of some kind, a shape, an outline. He stared in puzzlement, unable to make it out, and then strode over to get a closer view. Black cinders from the burned grass covered the cuffs of his trousers, rising up in a kind of sooty cloud as he walked. The acrid tang of the newly burned stems was so strong that his nostrils ached at the smell.

He was about fifty yards from the object and

perhaps a hundred yards from the dam when he stopped in his tracks and stared incredulously. Amazement, fear, hope, and bewilderment rushed over him in a wave as he recognized what it was. He hurried forward in a shambling run, his heart thumping painfully. It was Jodie's wheelchair, or what was left of it—a blackened frame, twisted and lying on its side, with the seat, upholstery, tires, battery leads and wiring all burned or melted away, but still clearly the remains of her wheelchair.

He knelt beside it for a moment and then stood up, staring about wide-eyed. As he did so he caught his breath, and the skin on the nape of his neck prickled strangely. There was the sound again, the bird call he had thought he heard up at the stables. But it was different now—nearer and clearer, less like a waterbird and more like a . . .

He started to run toward the high bank of the dam when the cry came again, a long wavering cry full of pain and helplessness. It was a human voice.

"Dad," it cried. "Dad-ee-ee-ee. He-e-e-lp."

With his mind reeling as if a rocket had exploded inside his head, he rushed down the track and raced up the steep bank.

"Jodie!" he yelled. As he neared the top, the hidden interior of the dam leaped into view.

"Jodie!" It was a shout, a question, a frantic yell of exultation.

She was lying in the mud near the edge, half in and half out of the water. She raised her head weakly. "Dad," she called again. "Help. Please help me."

He was at her side in an instant, floundering in the tacky bog, holding her by the shoulders and lifting with all his strength.

"Jodie," he kept saying over and over again. "Oh Jodie, Jodie, Jodie."

18

WHEN MONARCH reared away in fright and her wheelchair capsized, Jodie lay half stunned in the long grass by the side of the track. The air was stifling. Ash and surging smoke scudded over her, and a terrifying noise filled her ears—a strange tearing sound as if a thousand pieces of calico a mile long were being torn to shreds by a giant hand. It was the roar of the bushfire in the scrub near Thompsons' track.

She forced herself up on one elbow and looked about, dazed and desperate. Her eyes were smarting from the smoke and it was hard to see anything clearly in the blur, but she knew that the dam was only fifty or sixty yards down the slope. Using

146

her left arm to heave her shoulders off the ground, and thrusting wildly with her right heel, she forced herself forward in a series of painful lurches, like a novice swimmer using sidestroke. There were no longer separate places that hurt—elbows, hips, knees, or shoulders. The whole world was agony. Existence itself was pain. In her confused and semi-delirious state she half wondered whether the holocaust had already swept over her, engulfing her body and making it one with universal fire.

Yet something drove her on—a stubborn instinct, a will to survive. Pushing, heaving, scrabbling, and crawling through the smoke and heat, she slowly edged her way toward the dam, until at last, with the fiery fury less than a hundred yards away, she clawed her way to the top of the bank and, with a final desperate lurch, rolled down the steep inner slope into the water. There she lay half submerged while hell roared all around her and above her, and finally thundered away in a whirlwind of flame and ash toward the valley beyond. Whether she believed it or not, she was still alive.

The water and the mud that saved Jodie from the fire now became her enemy. As the storm of flame swept past and the hot cinders rained down on her, she crouched so low in the dam that she was covered almost to the chin. There was less water than mud — a tacky sludge that was thicker than porridge and as sticky as glue. She was up to her waist in it. She remembered her father saying that the dam needed a good cleaning out. Recently one of the Thompsons' runaway calves had got itself bogged down, and even strong horses and cattle sometimes had trouble when drinking there.

Floundering frantically, she finally managed to draw one leg out of the bog. The mud clung tenaciously right to the end, sucking off her sneaker as she pulled herself free. The pain in her hips and knees was brutal, and the struggle used up the last dregs of her strength. Using her free leg as a lever, she managed to push most of her body to the edge of the dam, but that was as far as she could go. She lay sprawled forward with her cheek pressed against the cinder-strewn dirt of the bank like someone fallen in battle, like a victim killed in some iniquitous war.

She lay there for a long time. Once, in a sort of delirium, she thought she was at school, sleeping with her arm forward and her head resting on the desk in Mrs. Stone's class. For hours she drifted in and out of wakefulness, with dreams and reality merging in a blur until at last evening began to fall and darkness set in. It wasn't until the sound

148

of an engine cut into her consciousness that she woke with a start and tried to heave herself up on one elbow. The engine ground its way up the drive toward the house. She saw the flare of the headlights sweep across the sky, but lying where she was in the hollow of the dam, she couldn't see anything more. She hoped against hope that it was her father and mother, and perhaps Alan, coming to check the place, although the vehicle sounded bigger and noisier than a car.

As soon as she heard the engine being switched off, and the distant thud of car doors slamming, she started calling as loudly as she could — a cooee followed by a long anguished cry. She wanted them to hear her before they went inside. It hadn't occurred to her that the house might no longer exist.

Her cries were all in vain. Nobody heard. No footsteps came hurrying down to investigate, no lights flashed in her direction. She called until she was hoarse. When the engine started once more and the sound slowly faded into the distance toward Greenvale, she fell forward again and sobbed uncontrollably. She felt utterly alone and rejected. She was too weak and wracked with pain to crawl, and there was no way in which she could make it to the top of the bank, let alone all the way back to the house. Nobody knew where she was. She was just another bit of flotsam left behind by the fury of the fire—a scrap of human debris.

And so the long night wore on. Sometimes she dozed off but woke up only too soon on the cold ground, with her body always in agony. She hadn't taken any pills or painkillers since morning and she had none in her pockets. She was hungry too, and her wet clothes were clammy and stinking of mud.

Sometimes she thought about Monarch. In her mind's eye she relived those last terrifying moments over and over again, when he had reared and plunged off at the sudden onrush of the stampeding horses, when she had clung to the rope and cried out to him, when the wheelchair had capsized and she had finally lost him. Where was he now? What had happened to him after he had followed the mob fleeing from the front of the fire? Her heart ached with a pain that was different from the pain in the rest of her body, and in some ways even more agonizing.

Toward morning she became feverish, shivering from exposure and weakness. Luckily she was sheltered from the wind in the basin of the dam. Luckily, too, she was spared the sight of the logs, trees, and remnants of houses still burning on the

150

slopes — glowing like red eyes in the darkness. And in the dam she was spared the sight of the ruins of her own home.

Out of the blur of semiconsciousness came the sound of another engine. She wasn't sure whether it was real or imagined. She listened without even trying to sit up — lying as she had all night with her head on the ground. Yes, she was sure it was another engine, a car coming up the drive toward the house. It was traveling slowly, almost halfheartedly it seemed to her, as if unsure of itself.

When it finally stopped, she guessed that it had reached the house. There was silence all around in the half-light — the silence of death. She propped herself up on one arm again, took a deep breath, and cried out desperately. She wanted it to be a call that would echo across the hillsides, but she was so weak that she was afraid it was no louder than the coo of a dove. She called again and again until she drooped forward from utter exhaustion.

A long silence followed. The light grew stronger and she was aware of the sky brightening from the imminent sun. Forcing herself by the sheer power of her will, she sat up dizzily and called again. Surely there was someone out there who could hear her? She suddenly had a strange conviction, a kind of premonition, that her father was

151

searching for her. He was sad and puzzled, but he was looking everywhere. Excitedly she changed her call.

"Dad," she cried. "Dad-ee-ee-ee. He-e-e-lp."

Miraculously there were footsteps beyond the bank of the dam. She could hear them thudding. They were silent for a moment, as if the person who made them had paused, looking, listening. She cried out once more. The footsteps started again, quickly this time, gathering speed. Someone was running hard.

"Dad," she called for the last time.

"Jodie!" She heard his voice and the hiss of his breath even before he reached the top of the bank. He was racing up the steep outer slope.

"Jodie!" he shouted again. A moment later he came dashing into view, silhouetted against the morning sky, and then rushed down the bank toward her.

19

ODIE'S FATHER ran all the way back to the car, carrying her in his arms. He said afterward that he didn't know how he found the strength to do it. Then he drove furiously to Greenvale and stopped in front of the hall.

He left Jodie lolling half asleep in the car while he dashed inside. Jodie's mother was standing up drowsily trying to comb her hair, wondering where her husband had got to. He came running up to her, unshaven and disheveled as he was, and seized her by the arms. She could see by his face that something unbelievable had happened.

"Jodie's alive!" he cried.

153

She reeled slightly and stared at him with her lips parted. She seemed to be frozen. He pressed her hands again as if trying to wake her up. "She's alive!" he repeated. "She's alive!"

"Alive?" Her voice was barely a whisper.

"Yes, yes."

"Is she . . . is she . . . ?"

"She's not burned. She hid in the dam. God knows how she got there. She's cold and exhausted and covered with mud, but she's all right. She's out in the car."

Jodie's mother let out a cry and started to run across the hall. A moment later she was hugging Jodie ecstatically, half in and half out of the car, laughing and crying, while the caked mud flaked off Jodie's arms and legs, and a small crowd of onlookers gathered around them with tears in their eyes.

An ambulance officer in the group finally interrupted their joy. He could see that Jodie was really half delirious. "I think we should get her to a doctor as soon as possible," he said. "She's suffering from exposure and shock. Unfortunately Dr. Manners and Dr. Harper have just gone home to bed. They've been up all night."

"We won't bother them," Jodie's father answered. "I'm going to contact Dr. Klein straight away. Her arthritis has flared up fearfully, so I think he'll put her in the hospital for a while."

"The ambulance is right here. I can take her down there now if you like."

"All right. I'll alert Dr. Klein and come with you."

By ten o'clock Jodie was back in her old hospital bed, washed clean and sedated, and wearing a borrowed nightgown that was five sizes too big for her. It flopped around her small body like a calico tent. Dr. Klein came in shortly afterward and stood eyeing her, partly in admiration and partly in amazement.

"Jodie Carpenter," he said, "you are the most incredible patient I've ever had."

She opened one eye drowsily. "Hullo, Dr. Klein."

"What on earth have you been up to? Carrying on in the middle of a bushfire, tumbling into dams, crawling about in the mud. You're supposed to be taking things easy."

Through the haze she knew he was teasing her. "I *am* taking it easy," she answered wryly, and closed her eyes again. Her arms were resting on the coverlet with her swollen knuckles and deformed fingers only too plain to see.

He walked over to the bedside and stood looking

down at her kindly. "Have a long sleep," he said. "Then we'll see how you feel."

She managed to open one of her drooping eyelids slightly. "My head's woozy," she answered, "and I feel lousy."

The story of Jodie's amazing survival made head-lines in the newspapers and was reported on radio and television. The people of Greenvale pressed her mother and father by the hands and thanked God for her escape. It was a miracle.

During the following days the vast cost of the inferno throughout the state became clear. More than two dozen people had lost their lives and dozens more were in hospitals. Almost two hun-dred houses had been destroyed, as well as many other buildings — some of them beautiful old places, rich in history. More than 300,000 sheep and 11,000 cattle had been burned to death, and another 300,000 sheep and 30,000 cattle that had survived now had nothing to eat. It was a catastrophe so huge that it was almost beyond understanding.

Gradually, temporary arrangements were made for all the people who were homeless, and the long bitter business of patching up their shattered lives began. Jodie's mother and father were invited to stay with Oscar Hoffmann for the time being, and they accepted gratefully. They had a big decision to make — whether to rebuild their house or leave the Hills forever.

"There's really no point in staying," Jodie's mother said. "And even if we do, there'll be more bushfires."

"That's a cheerful thought," said Jodie's father.

"We came up here mainly for Jodie's sake. But she can't ride anymore, and now even Monarch's gone. Maybe we'd be better off in town."

"Would we?"

"Don't you think so?"

"Not really."

"Why?"

"I guess I've got used to the open spaces, and the waterbirds on the dam, the magpies caroling, the kookaburras laughing in the morning. And the trees and grass."

Jodie's mother looked out at the blackened landscape all round. "The trees and the grass get burned."

"They grow again."

She sighed. "Well, if you're so keen." Then she brightened a little. "I guess if we stay here, I'll be able to design a new house."

"We'll see what Alan thinks, and especially Jodie when she comes out of the hospital.

Five days after the fire, they had a phone call at Oscar Hoffmann's place. It was from a man they had met once or twice at horse shows — a Mr. Harry Bennett, who owned a farm near Strathalbyn.

"That horse your daughter used to ride," he said to Jodie's father, "what was his name again?"

"Monarch."

"That's it, Monarch. A bay gelding?"

"Yes."

"With a white blaze on his nose?"

Jodie's father was excited. "That's right — a narrow white blaze. Why? Have you seen him?"

Mr. Bennett coughed. "I've got him right here. Found him with five or six other strays down in one of the creeks."

Jodie's father couldn't believe his ears. "That's wonderful," he shouted jubilantly. "My daughter will be over the moon."

"Better not say too much till you've seen him. He's in pretty bad shape."

A chill seemed to fall on Jodie's father. "In what way?"

"He's very lame. He must have gone through a

158

dozen fences, I reckon. He's cut about something awful. Some of the wounds have festered."

Jodie's father hesitated. "Is he going to be all right?"

"Don't know. I've called the vet, but he's so busy that he can't get down here till tonight. I'll do what I can."

"Thanks, Harry."

"He must be a real little rocket, you know, to outrun that fire. A lot of horses didn't make it."

"No."

"Well, I'll be in touch."

"Look, I'll come straight down, Harry. If I can, I'll bring a vet with me."

"Okay, that's fine."

Monarch's injuries were even worse than Jodie's father had feared. He had obviously crashed blindly through barbed wire fences and all kinds of other obstacles in his flight from the fire. He was covered with lacerations and open wounds, some of which were weeping and infected, and there was a deep cut near the stifle. The damage to his legs and fetlocks was so bad that he could only hobble.

At first the vet suggested that it might be better to put him down painlessly. Perhaps it would be kinder that way, not only for the horse but for

Jodie too, because she had really said good-bye to him on the day of the fire. "He'll never be able to compete in a show again," the vet said. "Nobody could ever ride him. He'll be lame for the rest of his life."

But Jodie's father wouldn't hear of it. "I'd never be able to face my daughter again," he said, "if I did a thing like that behind her back."

So they patched Monarch up as best they could and left him with Mr. Bennett, who was willing to board him for the time being. They didn't tell Jodie until she came home from the hospital, but then they all drove down to Strathalbyn to give her the most wonderful surprise of her life.

"Monarch!" She let out such a cry when she saw him that it echoed all around the farmyard. "Monarch. It's you. It's you."

Then she limped over toward him with a rush. He looked up and whinnied, and hobbled forward too. When they met he nuzzled her with his nose in the old way while she patted his neck breathlessly.

"You silly old duffer," she said between sobs. "Look what you've done to yourself."

But her joy at seeing him alive outweighed everything else. Her father gave her some sugar cubes, which he had put in his pocket purposely, and she held them out in her cupped hand as usual.

"We're a couple of old hopalongs," she said. "Two of a kind."

Her father laughed. "You'll have to be pensioned off, both of you."

Although he was joking, that was really what had to happen to Monarch. In good time the rains came and the Hills were green once more. The blackened trees miraculously put out tiny shoots as they came to life again.

"Australian trees really are a miracle," a visitor from Europe said. "However did they survive a fire like that?"

Jodie's father smiled. "They've been practicing for millions of years."

On her first day back at school Jodie was surprised when Amanda Ritchie came up to her and said how glad she was to hear about Monarch, even though he would never compete again. At least he was alive. Amanda had lost Superior in the fire, just as half the Pony Club members — and girls like Tanya, who relied on other people — had lost their horses. At one blow the lives of most of the girls had been changed forever.

Jodie's heart went out to Amanda over the loss of Superior. She knew what she must be feeling.

She watched sadly as Amanda walked away across the yard, wondering why they should have disliked each other so much in the past. She decided that sometimes it needed a great natural tragedy to make people forget their jealousies and bring them together.

Jodie was able to get about a little better now. She was "in remission," as Dr. Klein called it. The pain was not quite as bad as it had been, and some new pills he had recommended seemed to be improving her mobility. He said that the doctors would soon be able to operate on the worst of her joints and give her still more movement.

"Will I be able to ride again?" she asked.

He shook his head. "No. Especially not if you have artificial hips."

"When will I have those?"

"One day, no doubt."

"Oh."

"But I think you'll be able to do many other things."

She stuck out her chin. "I'm sure I will."

He smiled. "So am I."

The house and the stables were rebuilt at last, and toward the end of the year they were able to move back home. They brought Monarch up from

Mr. Bennett's place at Strathalbyn in a borrowed trailer and turned him loose in his own paddock. He hobbled about happily, sniffing every tussock and post.

"There you are, boy," Jodie's father called. "What could be better than lazy days for the rest of your life?"

Jodie limped over to shut the gate. Her father watched her for a minute with a warm smile. "You know, Jodie," he said, "you and Monarch are certainly soul mates. You even walk the same way."

She turned cheekily and gave him a raspberry with her thumb. Then she joined him and they went back slowly up the track toward the house.

20

JODIE is nineteen now. She has had several operations and can walk reasonably well for short distances. She can even drive a car. She has finished a course in office management and has found a job as a receptionist at the front desk of a government department.

She is still small — over an inch short of five feet — but people call her petite. They like her lively face and dark expressive eyes. She is still in pain most of the day, of course, but people rarely know about it, even when she has to stand about at meetings and receptions until her body feels as if it is on fire. Eventually she moves away quietly and sits on a chair in the corner, but even then she is not lonely. Lots of people, especially young men, seem to want to talk to her.

In her spare time she acts as secretary of the Greenvale Pony Club. She enjoys the work very much, arranging competitions and outings, organizing training schools in dressage and show jumping, teaching young girls how to care for a horse and groom it properly. On Saturdays she is always out at a horse show or meet of one kind or another. Already people are saying that in a few years she could be a member of the executive committee of the Equestrian Federation, responsible for national events all over Australia.

She is also a member of the Arthritis Foundation. She works hard with other volunteers, raising money for research so that scientists can increase their understanding of the disease and perhaps one day discover the cause and the cure, so that nobody in the world need ever suffer its agonies again.

Of course she still has Monarch. He limps about contentedly in the paddock and gets fatter every day. When she comes home each afternoon, he is always waiting for her, whinnying excitedly. Jodie's mother laughs. "If we open the front door," she says, "that horse will be inside in a flash, sitting in one of the living-room chairs."

"And why not?" Jodie answers. "He's my very

best friend — it's just that he's shaped like a horse."

Jodie also talks to groups of young people who suffer from arthritis. She tells jokes and emphasizes her points with gestures and a quick smile.

"You can't afford to give up," she tells them. "You have to get on top of it, or it'll get on top of you."

The audiences listen attentively. They know Jodie Carpenter's story. But when they applaud her, she waves their praises aside with a smile and says, "It's just a journey you have to make." Then she grins and adds, "But sometimes the journey's a bit rough."

A Note from the Publisher

Having got this far, readers might be interested to discover a little about how and why *Jodie's Journey* came to be written. The book itself has undergone a journey of its own, and its story is worth telling.

Colin Thiele, who is Vice-Patron of the Arthritis Foundation of South Australia, knows something of the cruel effects of rheumatoid arthritis, as he himself has suffered severely from this disease for almost forty years.

As one of Australia's most popular children's authors, he receives thousands of letters from young readers every year. In 1987 an eleven-year-old girl named Sharyn Stevens, from South Croydon, Victoria, wrote to him about her problem:

Recently I read an article about you in a magazine and I noticed the part that said that you write your novels while in hospital with arthritis. I was wondering if you would be able to write a story about a child with arthritis, the reason being that I suffer from arthritis too. My friends don't seem to understand why I can't run or play lots of games they play, and by you writing this book maybe they and some other people will understand.

Sharyn's plea was one Colin Thiele appreciated and understood. After much thought he began work on *Jodie's Journey*. His daughter Sandy — an avid rider — supplied much of the information about the care and training of horses and the conduct of show-jumping championships, but the details about arthritis came from his own firsthand knowledge and through the help of Charmain Hodge, another young sufferer.

The first draft of the manuscript was given to Dr. Stephen Milazzo, a leading specialist in rheumatology, who has treated Colin Thiele for many years. He read it all carefully to check the accuracy

168

of its medical content and made many valuable comments on it.

The author and publisher wish to thank each of these people for their help and interest, and especially Sharyn for suggesting the idea in the first place and for permitting us to reproduce part of her letter here.

Finally, the author wishes to assure readers that, although the Ash Wednesday bushfires of February 1983 really did happen as described, and large areas of the beautiful Adelaide Hills really were devastated, Greenvale itself does not exist and its inhabitants are all fictitious . . . in case you were wondering.